Made in heaven

"I don't in any way see a marriage between us as being second-best—far from it. In fact, in my view . . . " Stuart stopped and then said more calmly, "I've already said that I don't want to pressure you. At least we can be sure of one thing," he added, turning away from her slightly. "There can be no doubt that sexually we're going to be extremely compatible."

How on earth did he know that? How on earth *could* he know that? Sara opened her mouth to ask him and then closed it again, conscious of a naiveté and self-consciousness that tied her tongue and kept her silent, while her pulse raced and a sensation like a tiny jolt of electricity burned through her body. . . .

PENNY JORDAN was constantly in trouble in school because of her inability to stop daydreaming—especially during French lessons. In her teens, she was an avid romance reader, although it didn't occur to her to try writing one herself until she was older. "My first half-dozen attempts ended up ingloriously," she remembers, "but I persevered, and one manuscript was finished." She plucked up the courage to send it to a publisher, convinced her book would be rejected. It wasn't, and the rest is history! Penny is married and lives in Cheshire.

Penny Jordan's striking mainstream novel *Power Play* quickly became a *New York Times* bestseller. She followed that success with *Silver*, a story of ambition, passion and intrigue and *The Hidden Years*, a novel that lays bare the choices all women face in their search for love.

Don't miss Penny's latest blockbuster, *Lingering Shadows*, available in August.

Books by Penny Jordan

HARLEQUIN PRESENTS
1476—SECOND TIME LOVING
1491—PAYMENT DUE
1508—A FORBIDDEN LOVING
1529—A TIME TO DREAM
1544—DANGEROUS INTERLOPER

PENNY JORDAN

Second-best Husband

Harlequin Books

TORONTO • NEW YORK • LONDON
AMSTERDAM • PARIS • SYDNEY • HAMBURG
STOCKHOLM • ATHENS • TOKYO • MILAN
MADRID • WARSAW • BUDAPEST • AUCKLAND

Harlequin Presents first edition May 1993
ISBN 0-373-11552-0

Original hardcover edition published in 1991
by Mills & Boon Limited

SECOND-BEST HUSBAND

CHAPTER ONE

'So you've actually done it, then? You've handed in your notice and left?'

'Yes,' Sara agreed in a low voice, flinching a little as though hearing the words physically pained her.

Her friend and neighbour grimaced sympathetically. She was ten years older than Sara and had known her ever since Sara had bought the house next to their own four years before, and personally she felt like giving a very, very loud cheer. Ian Saunders, Sara's boss, might be six feet odd of blond good-looking manhood, all outward charm and attractiveness, but inwardly he was as cold and callous as it was possible for a man to be. That was *her* considered opinion, but in the past, no matter how many times she had voiced it, Sara had refused to listen to her, to hear a word against the man she worked for and loved.

'Well, you know what I think,' she told Sara now. 'For what it's worth, I consider that leaving is the best thing you could have done.'

Sara's mouth twisted sadly. She was a tall, slender woman of twenty-nine, with a quiet, calm manner that masked a keenly efficient brain. Her looks mirrored her personality. Her face was delicately oval in shape, her features elegant and well-proportioned, only her mouth, with its unexpected fullness, hinting that her outward control might mask deep and fiery passions.

'It wasn't exactly a calm and reasoned decision made of my own free will.'

The pain in her voice made Margaret, her neighbour, turn her head away from her in angry sympathy.

How *could* Ian Saunders have treated Sara so badly after all she had done for him, working for him like a slave, helping him to build up his business into the success it was today, and all the time loving him, hoping...? Although Sara had always been openly honest in her own knowledge that Ian didn't return her love, privately Margaret suspected he must have surely guessed how she felt, and, having guessed, out of compassion and concern ought to have suggested years ago that it might be wiser for Sara to find a job elsewhere. Instead of which he had allowed an intimacy to develop between them, a closeness, even if that relationship had been completely non-sexual, which had held out just enough unspoken promise, just enough allure, to make poor Sara go on hoping that maybe one day a miracle *would* occur and that he would turn to her... want her... need her... not as his faithful PA but as a woman, his woman.

Instead of which he had calmly walked into his office a week ago and announced that he was getting engaged and that he would soon be married.

Sara had been devastated, but when she, Margaret, had urged her then to hand in her notice and make a new life for herself she had selflessly refused, shaking her head, pointing out that if she left it would damage the business which Ian had worked so hard to build up.

'You were right,' Sara was saying unhappily now. 'I should have had the sense to hand in my notice when Ian told me that he and Anna were getting married. But, like the blind fool that I was, I had no idea that Anna wanted my job as well as . . .' She broke off, swallowing painfully.

It wasn't like her to unburden herself like this, but what had happened yesterday had upset and distressed her so much . . .

She had gone to work as usual. Ian had been away seeing one of their clients, and, although she had felt wary and uncomfortable at first when Anna walked into the office, she had had no idea of the real purpose of the other woman's visit until Anna had launched into the speech which had ultimately led to Sara's acknowledging that for her own sake she had to make the break from Ian and forge a completely new life for herself well away from him.

'What exactly did she say to you?' Margaret pressed gently, sensing Sara's need to unburden herself.

They were sitting in Sara's neat, spotless kitchen. Margaret had called round to see her, alerted to the fact that something must be wrong by the fact that Sara had arrived home from work halfway through the afternoon and, after parking her car haphazardly in front of the house, had practically run inside.

Margaret had followed her, anxious to discover what was wrong and if there was anything she could do to help.

Sara shrugged, bending her head over the mug of coffee she was nursing. Her hair was straight and silky, a soft, pretty fair colour which she had expertly highlighted and styled into an elegant shoulder-length bob, which added to her air of competence and efficiency.

Margaret, who had seen her when she was at home, doing her housework, her hair tied up in a pony-tail, her face free of make-up, had been surprised to discover how very young and vulnerable it had made her look, how very much more approachable.

'More sexy,' Ben, her husband, had corrected her with a grin. Margaret had frowned him down, even while she acknowledged that it was true. Sara might know how to present herself to make herself look efficient, but when it came to presenting herself in a way that made men...

She gave a small sigh; as a modern woman it went against the grain to suggest to another member of her sex that she ought deliberately to focus on those facets of her looks and personality which made her look more vulnerable and less efficient, and yet she knew how much Sara, for all her efficiency, longed for children, a family... When she spoke of her elder sister, and her two children and another on the way, her face softened and her eyes turned from blue to violet...

As Sara stared into the brown depths of her coffee, she gave a tiny shudder.

What had Anna said? Margaret had asked her. Even now she could hardly endure to recall exactly what Anna Thomas had said to her when she had walked into Ian's office, red lips pouting, her white-blonde hair a mass of untidy tousled curls, her skirt surely too short and tight ... And yet obviously *Ian* found her attractive. Far more so than ... Sara swallowed, forcing herself to block out her emotions and to concentrate instead on answering Margaret's question.

'Well, basically, she simply pointed out to me that both she and Ian were aware of my... my feelings for him, that in fact they'd both derived quite a lot of amusement from the fact that I obviously thought I'd managed to keep them hidden. As she pointed out, there's nothing quite as pathetic as a secretary in love with her boss, especially when there's absolutely no chance of his returning her feelings.'

She paused as Margaret made a small sound of shocked anger, and shook her head.

'Well, it's true enough, even though I had rather flattered myself that Ian and I were more partners than boss and secretary.'

'Partners!' Margaret interrupted explosively, unable to control herself any longer. 'Why, *you* virtually *ran* that business for him! Without you...'

Sara smiled sadly at her.

'I wish it was true, but in all honesty it was Ian's salesmanship, his flair that made the business a success. I merely worked in the background. Anyway, to continue, as Anna pointed out to me, it would hardly be in my best interests to stay on with Ian now that they were getting married; she could easily replace me in the office, and she and Ian had decided that it would be better all round if I looked for another job. She did say that I could stay until the end of the month if I wished.'

Sara paused, the wry self-contempt in her voice making Margaret wince for her.

'What could I do? Naturally I told her I'd be leaving immediately. That was yesterday. I only went in today to clear my desk, to tidy up a few odds and ends...'

She bit her lip. She was trying hard not to break down. It had been such an extraordinary interview, so unexpected, so hurtful, when she had believed that she had already suffered all the hurt she could possibly endure.

She had *known* that Ian was seeing Anna, of course, just as she had known about all the other women he had dated in the ten years during which she had worked for him. She had been devastated when he'd told her that he was marrying Anna, but she'd thought she had managed to conceal her feelings from him, just as she had believed that he had never once, in all the years she had worked for him, guessed about the hopes she cherished, the love she felt for him.

She had honestly believed that Margaret was the only person who knew how she felt, and only because, the year after Sara had moved in next door to her, Margaret had come round unexpectedly one evening and found her in tears because Ian had cancelled the evening out he had arranged for the two of them, as their 'Christmas party' and a thank-you to her for all her hard work during the year, so that he could go instead to a party with his latest girlfriend.

Not even her parents or her sister knew... or at least she assumed they didn't, and she wondered miserably now if even they *had* guessed, and had kept silent out of pity and compassion for her.

She was fully deserving of the contempt Anna had poured on her, she reflected bitterly now. She was, after all, that most ridiculous of stereotyped creatures, the dull, plain woman, desperately in love with her charming, handsome boss... But at least now she had broken out of that mould by handing in her notice.

'Well, if you want my advice, you're well out of it,' Margaret told her roundly, adding equally forthrightly, 'All right, I know you hate anyone criticising Ian, but for once I'm going to say what I think, and that is that he's used you, used your talents, your skills, and now——'

'And now that he's fallen in love with Anna there isn't any room in his life for me any more,' Sara interrupted her quietly. 'And to think that all this time I honestly believed I'd successfully hidden how I felt. At first, when I got that job with him... well, I was only nineteen, my head stuffed with dreams.' She was talking more to herself than to her friend.

'I'd come to London from Shropshire because I wanted to improve my skills, my chances of getting a top-class job. My parents were concerned about my leaving home, but they didn't try to stop me. At first I was thoroughly miserable... thoroughly homesick. I was sharing a place with three other girls, working as a temp during the day, and going to college at night to improve my computer and language skills, and then I met Ian. He was taking the same computer course. He was twenty-five then, and he had just broken away and set up his own business. He was a salesman really, he told me, and what he really needed desperately was someone to run the office for him. Eventually he offered me the job, and I jumped at it. He was always a generous boss financially...and then, when Gran died, I used the money I inherited from her to buy this place. I wasn't homesick any more...I'd made friends, made a life here for myself, and, if I couldn't bear to admit it to anyone else, I had already admitted to myself that it was my love for Ian as much as the challenge of my job that kept me working for him. Like a fool, I never gave up hoping...'

And he allowed you to have that hope, Margaret thought shrewdly, but didn't say so. She felt that Sara had endured more than enough already without having any more burdens to carry.

'So what will you do now?' she asked gently.

'Go home,' Sara told her, smiling wryly when she saw Margaret's expression.

'Yes, silly, isn't it? I'm a grown woman of twenty-nine, who's lived in London for ten years, and yet for some reason I still think of Shropshire as home. I've got quite a bit saved...I can let this place if necessary...I can afford to take a few months off, give myself time...' She shook her head uncomfortably, aware that one of the reasons she was so intent on leaving London was because she was afraid—afraid that, once her initial shock and the anger that went with it had gone, she would become vulnerably weak...that she would find excuses for getting in touch with Ian—small matters outstanding at the office...small facts which only she knew—and she didn't want to allow herself to degenerate into that kind of helpless self-destructiveness. Things were bad enough as it was, without her making them worse...without her knowingly allowing herself to hang on to the coat-tails of Ian's life, pathetic and unwanted, an object of derision and contempt.

She closed her eyes as her vision became blurred by tears, obliterating the mental image she had just had of Ian and Anna together, laughing about her, Ian's handsome blond head flung back, his blue eyes laughing, his expression one of callous contempt. She shivered suddenly, acknowledging how odd it was that she was able to conjure up that image so easily; and yet, had anyone ever suggested to her that Ian could be callous, could be cruel, could be deliberately malicious and unkind, she would have refuted their criticisms immediately. Except . . . over the years there had been occasions, moments, when even her devotion had wavered, flinching a little as he made a decision, a comment, a pronouncement which she had soft-heartedly felt to be less warm and generous than it should have been.

She had known always that he was egotistical, but she had allowed herself to believe it was the egotism of a spoiled little boy who didn't know any better, who would never deliberately inflict cruelty on others. Had she been wrong? Had she all this time refused to allow herself to see the truth? She shivered again, causing Margaret to watch her with some concern.

Despite Sara's outward air of competence and self-containment, her neighbour had always privately thought that these only narrowly masked an inner vulnerability and fragility, a soft femininity which made Margaret despise Ian Saunders even more for his lack of concern and compassion for her friend.

'Yes, I think you should go home,' she said firmly now. 'Even though I know I'm going to miss you desperately, especially when I'm looking for someone to look after those two awful brats of mine.'

Sara laughed shakily. 'You know you adore them,' she countered.

'Mmm...but I try not to let *them* guess it. It's hard work at times being the only woman in a household of three males.' She paused and then said quietly, 'I know this probably isn't the time to raise this particular subject, but I'm going to say something to you that I've wanted to say for a long time. I'm older than you, Sara, and I've seen a lot more of life. I know how you feel about Ian Saunders, or at least how you think you feel, but in all honesty you've never allowed yourself to discover whether you could allow yourself to love or care for any other man, have you?' she asked gently.

'Allow myself——' Sara began, but Margaret refused to let her speak.

'Falling in love is easy, *loving* someone is a lot harder; and going on loving them, through the nitty-gritty of mundane everyday life, is even harder, *and* even more worthwhile.

'I know from the things you've told me, from watching you with my own two, that you want children. You know what you should do now, don't you? You should put Ian Saunders right out of your mind and look round for a nice man to marry and have those children with.'

Sara couldn't help it. She flushed defensively. 'I *can't* switch off my feelings just like that, marry a man I don't love, no matter how much I might want a family.'

Of course Margaret was right. Of course she wanted children. Sometimes, in fact, that wanting was so sharp, so acutely painful that it made her ache inside, made her wake up at night . . . but what Margaret was telling her to do was impossible.

'I wasn't in love with Ben when I married him,' Margaret told her softly, astounding Sara. She had never met anyone apart from her own parents who were as devoted and as obviously content and happy together as her neighbours, and she had always assumed that they had been deeply in love when they married. 'And, what's more, *he* wasn't in love with *me*. In fact, we were both on the rebound from other relationships. We'd known each other some time in a casual, friendly sort of way. One evening we got talking . . . we discovered how many interests we had in common, including a desire to settle down and raise a family, and that those needs had not been shared by our previous partners, the ones with whom we were so much in love. So we talked about it, started going out together, to see if it . . . if *we* could work, and then, when we found that we were getting on as well together as we had hoped, we got married. Not because we were in love, but because we both genuinely and honestly thought we could make our relationship work. I've never for one minute regretted that decision, and I don't think Ben has either—and do you know something else?' She gave Sara a shining, almost defensive smile. 'I don't know quite how it has happened, but somehow there's been a small miracle for both of us, and now we love one another very much indeed.'

'I envy you, Margaret, but I don't think...'

'Listen to me. You and I are very much alike in many ways. Stop wasting your life on a man who you can't have and who would hurt you badly if you could. *Don't* spend the rest of your life weeping tears of regret. Decide what it is you really want. Use this time with your parents at home to think about the things which are really important to you. All right, so you may decide that I'm wrong, that a husband, a home, a family aren't the things you want enough to put aside your dreams of falling in love, of *being* in love for. But on the other hand you might find you make some surprising discoveries about yourself and about your true needs.'

As Sara turned off the motorway and took the familiar route homewards, she found herself turning over in her mind what Margaret had said to her. A home...children... Yes, these were things she had always wanted. Despite her decision to move to London, to carve a life for herself as a career woman in the big city, at heart she had remained the small-town girl she had been born. She had enjoyed her years in London, but in her heart of hearts she had never believed they would be anything other than a busy interlude between her childhood and her eventual role as a wife and mother.

Every time she saw her parents, every time she saw her sister, she was reminded of her most basic needs and how her life was stifling them. How it was stifling her. But she hadn't been able to bring

herself to break away from Ian . . . She had refused
to make herself face up to the truth: that there never
was going to come a day when he *would* turn to
her, look at her . . . take her in his arms. She was
twenty-nine years old. Not old by any means, but
no longer young enough to deceive herself with such
silly daydreams. She thought of the men who had
asked her out over the years, kind, pleasant men,
but just men when compared with Ian, with her
love, her adoration . . . her compulsive worship of
him. Men whom she had refused, ignored, forgotten . . . Men with whom, according to Margaret,
she could easily have been happy and fulfilled . . . men with whom she could have had
children. Children who would have given her so
much joy—children who would have made her
forget Ian? Impossible, surely . . . or was it simply
that she did not *want* to allow herself to forget him;
that she was so conscious of the fact that she had
wasted so much of her life, given up so much, to
maintain her devotion to him, that her pride, her
stubbornness, would not allow her to admit that
she had made a mistake, had behaved in a stupid
blinkered fashion? But now that she was being
forced into separating her life from his . . . now that
she . . .

She moved restlessly in her seat. Her back was
beginning to ache from the long drive. She was glad
that it was almost summer and the evenings light
enough to allow her to complete her journey before
it grew dark.

Her expression softened into one of warm
affection as she thought about her parents. Her
father was retired now. He and her mother still lived

in the house where she and her sister had grown up, though. Two miles outside the village, it stood alone, halfway down a lane which led eventually to the Jacobean manor house whose home farm it had once been.

The manor house had been empty for several years, the old man who had owned it having died and there being no direct heir, nor apparently anyone interested in purchasing such a rambling and derelict property so far off the beaten track. But when she had last been home at Christmas—Ian had booked a skiing holiday in Colorado for Christmas and the New Year, and so there had been nothing to tempt her to stay in London, even if she could have brought herself to disappoint her parents and break with family tradition by doing so—her mother had told her excitedly that the house had at last been sold. The man who had bought it was some sort of tree expert with the Forestry Commission who had now decided to branch out into a business of his own, growing and selling not only rare specimen trees, but also many native broad-leaved trees, for which apparently there was a growing market both at home and abroad in these environmentally aware days.

Her parents had only met their new neighbour briefly, but Sara had gained the impression that her mother had rather taken him to her heart.

'All on his own living in that great draughty place,' was what she had said at Christmas, adding that she had invited him to join them for Christmas Day, but that he had apparently already made arrangements to spend the holiday with friends in the north-east of the country.

'He's not married, and has no family to speak of. Both his parents are dead, and his brother lives in Australia.'

How like her mother to wheedle so much information out of a stranger so very quickly, Sara reflected fondly. Not out of nosiness; her mother wasn't like that. She was one of those people who was naturally concerned for and caring about her fellow men.

What would she have made of Ian had Sara ever taken him home? It came to her with a small unpleasant jolt of surprise that she knew without even having to consider the matter that her parents would not have taken to Ian; that he in turn would have treated them with that slightly disdainful contempt she had seen him use to such effect with anyone he considered neither important enough nor interesting enough to merit his attention.

She bit her lip, worrying at it without realising what she was doing.

But Ian wasn't really like that. He was fun, clever, quick-witted...not...not shallow, vain and self-important. Or was he? Had she in her love for him been guilty of wearing rose-coloured glasses, of seeing in him the qualities she *wanted* to see and ignoring those which reflected less well on him, which actually existed?

If he was really the man she had wanted to believe he was, had *allowed* herself to believe he was, would he have been attracted to a woman like Anna, outwardly attractive in an obvious and rather overdone sort of way, but inwardly...?

Sara bit her lip again. She had no right to criticise Anna just because she... No doubt Ian saw a side of her that wasn't discernible to her, another woman...a woman moreover who loved him. Jealousy wasn't an attractive emotion, and *she* was hardly an impartial critic, she reminded herself sternly. And, anyway, what did it matter what she thought of Anna? *Ian* loved her. He had told her so himself.

Her body tensed as she remembered that awful day. A Monday morning. Ian had been away for the weekend to stay with 'friends'. To stay with Anna, she had realised later. He had arrived halfway through the morning glowing with enthusiasm and excitement.

It had happened at last, he had told Sara exuberantly. He had at last met the woman with whom he wanted to spend the rest of his life...a woman like no other...

She remembered how she had listened, sick at heart, her body still as she forbade it to reveal the anguish she was suffering, her face averted from him as she fought to control her shock, her pain.

And then, when she had actually met Anna for the first time, she had realised what a fool she had been to ever imagine that Ian might come to love her. She and Anna were so completely different from one another. She was tall and slim, thin almost; Anna was shorter, and all voluptuous curves. She was shy, withdrawn almost, quiet and rather reserved; Anna was a self-publicist with no inhibitions about singing her own praises, advancing her own talents.

Where she preferred restraint, quiet clothes in classic colours and styles, Anna wore the kind of expensive designer outfits calculated to draw people's attention.

Watching the way Ian looked at her, seeing the desire, the admiration in his eyes as he followed Anna's every movement, Sara had recognised how truly foolish she had been in ever allowing herself to hope that there might come a day when Ian would turn to her, would look at her.

She was simply not his type. Oh, he might *like* her... he might praise her work, he might even flatter her as he had done over the years... and she might have been silly enough to use that flattery to build herself a tower of hope that any sensible woman would soon have realised had no foundation at all; but the reality was that, whether Anna had arrived in his life or not, Ian would never have found her, Sara, desirable.

Face it, she derided herself bitterly now. You just aren't the kind of woman that men do desire.

She remembered how often her sister had teased her about her aloofness, had told her that she ought to relax more, have fun... 'You always look so prim and proper,' Jacqui had told her. 'So neat and perfect that no man would ever dare to ruffle your hair or smudge your lipstick.'

She had wanted to protest then that that wasn't true, but had been too hurt to do so. It wasn't her fault if she wasn't the curly, pretty, vivacious type.

She cringed inwardly, remembering how Anna had mocked her, telling her, 'Honestly, you're unbelievable. Quite the archetypal frustrated spinster type, dotingly in love with a man she can never have. I suppose you're still even a virgin. Ian thinks it's a huge joke, a woman of your age who hasn't had a lover; but then, as he said, what red-blooded man would want you?'

Anna had smiled a cruel little smile as she casually threw these comments to her, malice glinting in her light blue eyes as they focused on Sara's pale, set face.

Now, as she recalled her comments, Sara's hands tightened on the steering-wheel, her knuckles gleaming white with tension. Up until this moment, she hadn't allowed herself to think about that. To think about Anna and Ian—Ian whom she had loved so much and for so long—laughing about her, making fun of her.

She shuddered sickly, a rigour of tension and pain, and yet in the middle of her anguish there was still room for a small, cold voice that asked why, when she had had such a high opinion of Ian, she was not immediately and instantly rejecting the very idea that he would be so cruel, so callous about *anyone*? Never mind about *her*, someone whom he had known for so long, someone whom he had claimed to admire and care about.

She could accept that he couldn't love her; why should he? Love wasn't something that could be summoned on demand, nor banished equally easily, as she had good cause to know; but surely the Ian she had admired and liked so much, the Ian she had thought she had known so well, would never, ever have made fun of her, laughed so cruelly and tauntingly about her with anyone, even if that person was the woman he was going to marry. Surely the Ian she had thought she had known would have had the consideration, the kindness, the sheer compassion for even those members of the

human race who were not known to him personally
not to be able to entertain such small-mindedness.

The Ian she had *thought* she had known, even if
he had known about her feelings, her love, would
never have been able to behave in the way that Anna
had described to her, and yet, when Anna had
thrown her taunts at her, instead of immediately
and automatically being able to rebuff them as
being totally unworthy of Ian, totally impossible
for a man of his calibre, all she had been able to
do was to stand there sickly acknowledging the
extent of her own folly, her own self-deceit.

And yet even now it wasn't Ian she hated. It
wasn't Ian she despised.

No, those bitter, acid emotions were reserved for
herself. Which was why she had had to come away.
She dared not allow herself to weaken, to become
even more foolish and contemptible by staying in
London where it would be all too fatally easy to
find some excuse to make contact with Ian . . . some
excuse . . . any excuse . . . and she wasn't going to allow
that to happen. *Dared* not allow that to happen.

Thank goodness she had her parents to come
home to. They knew nothing about her feelings for
Ian; her mother always asked her about her life in
London, about whether or not she had met 'anyone
special', and Sara knew how disappointed she was
that she too hadn't married and had children, like
her sister—not because she wanted more grand-
children but because she knew how much Sara
herself loved them.

She glanced at her watch. Soon she would be
home. Only another few miles to Wrexall, the
village where she had been brought up. She loved

this part of the country with its rolling hills, its views of the distant Welsh borders. Ludlow with its historic past wasn't very far away, and she had grown up on the legends and myths of the countryside's old and bloody history.

Until his retirement, her father had been a partner in a solicitors' practice in Ludlow. It had been working in his office in the school holidays which had first given her the enthusiasm to train as a secretary. Her original ambition had been to perfect her languages and then to work abroad, possibly in Brussels, but then she had met Ian and everything had changed, and it was too late now to wonder what her life might have been if their paths had never crossed.

As she drove through the quiet village it was just growing dusk, lights coming on in the cottages that lined the road.

An anticipatory feeling warmed her heart, momentarily dispelling the aching coldness which had invaded it recently. No matter how mature she was supposed to be, she had never lost the feeling of happiness she always experienced at coming home.

Not even working for Ian had totally compensated her for seeing so little of her parents, her sister, her old friends—although most of her schoolfriends had moved away now; this part of the country couldn't provide them with the means to earn a satisfactory living. And her sister had moved away as well. She and her husband now lived in Dorset.

As she turned off the main road and into the lane that led to her parents' house, she felt her eyes sting a little. Heavens, the last thing she wanted to do was to break down in tears the moment she saw her parents. If she did that, her mother was bound to guess that something was wrong. She might have come home to lick her wounds, so to speak, but she fully intended to lick them in private.

She turned in through the open gates and drove up to the house, frowning a little as she saw that no lights were on, and then shrugging to herself. Her parents were probably in the kitchen. Her mother would be preparing supper and her father would be sitting at the kitchen table reading his evening paper.

Smiling to herself, she stopped her car and got out, hurrying down the side of the house.

However, when she turned the corner, there was no light on in the kitchen, no sign of life anywhere, and, worse, the garage door was open and her parents' car was missing.

Could they perhaps have gone shopping? She frowned to herself, chewing on her bottom lip. Unlikely, surely...

She was just beginning to wonder where on earth they could be when she heard the sound of a car coming up the lane.

However, as she hurried back to the front of the house, her relief evaporated as she saw that the vehicle which was now stationary at the bottom of the drive wasn't her parents' sedate saloon car, but a battered Land Rover.

The man swinging himself out of it was unfamiliar to her. Tall and powerfully built, with thick dark hair which looked as though it was overdue for a cut, he was frowning as he saw her.

He was wearing a pair of faded, worn jeans, ripped over one knee, and an equally ancient checked shirt. His Wellington boots were muddy and so were his hands, Sara noticed as he came towards her and told her, 'If you're looking for the Brownings, I'm afraid you're out of luck. They've gone to Dorset. Apparently their daughter went into premature labour late yesterday afternoon, and their son-in-law asked if they could possibly get down there to help out...'

He stopped abruptly, his frown deepening as he demanded, 'You aren't going to faint, are you?'

Faint? Her? Sara gave him a quelling, icy look. Never in her life had anyone accused her before of looking like the kind of woman who was likely to faint. In any other circumstances she might almost have found the fact that he had so obviously misjudged her slightly amusing. Men usually found her efficiency, her self-sufficiency rather off-putting, and the suggestion that he considered her weak and vulnerable enough to resort to something so ridiculously Victorian as fainting simply because her parents weren't here made her reflect inwardly that, whatever else this man was, he was certainly no expert on the female sex.

'No, I'm not going to faint,' she told him crisply. 'I was just rather shocked to discover that my parents aren't here.'

'Your parents!' He had been about to turn away, but now he swung round again and studied her with open curiosity. 'You're *Sara*!' he pronounced at last, looking at her with such obvious bewilderment that Sara wondered what on earth he had been told about her to make him view the reality of her with so much obvious disbelief.

'Yes, I'm Sara,' she agreed coolly, and then, remembering that she was back home now and not in London and that there was no need for her to be defensive and withdrawn, and moreover that this man was obviously well known to her parents, she added, 'And you must be...'

'Stuart Delaney,' he told her, extending his hand, and then withdrawing it as they both looked at the mud encrusting it. 'I've just been heeling in some young trees. I was on my way back home to get cleaned up when I saw your car. I knew your folks were away and so I thought I'd better just stop and take a look. Did they know you were...?'

Sara shook her head.

'No, I...' She broke off, unwilling to explain that her return home had been an impulse decision.

So this was her parents' new neighbour, the man who had bought the old manor house. He was younger than she had expected, somewhere in his early thirties, she judged, a tough-looking individual and yet one who evidently had far more neighbourliness in him than his appearance had led her to suspect, if he had been concerned enough to stop and see who was visiting her parents' home.

'Well, I'd better be on my way, then. You've got a key for the house, have you? Only your parents left a spare with me...'

'Yes, I've got my own key,' Sara assured him, thinking again how deceptive appearances could be. From the look of him she would hardly have expected him to be concerned about her, or about anyone else for that matter. He looked too hard, too remote...not like Ian, who looked so much more human, so much more approachable. And yet, in the same circumstances, would Ian have concerned himself about the possible plight of a stranger?

She started to turn away from him, aware that she was suddenly shockingly close to tears. To have come so far and then found that her parents weren't here. Only now was she prepared to admit how much she had counted on their being at home...on the soothing balm of their love, their quiet, unfussy concern, their...their presence. Well, it was far too late now to turn her car round and drive back to London, even if she had wanted to do so, which she did not. But the prospect of spending the night in an empty house with nothing to do other than fight against dwelling morbidly on everything that had happened... She started to move towards the house, and then blinked as the gravel beneath her feet started to heave and roll in the most peculiar way, rather as though it were water and not gravel at all. She was feeling oddly light-headed as well, and an irritated male voice seemed to be calling her name, but it came from so far away that it was little more than a dull rumble, like hearing sound through a seashell. Even so, she tried to respond to it, to turn in its direction, but everything was going dark...black... Too late she recognised that it had perhaps not been sensible of her not to have eaten anything before she left London earlier in the day, but she had been in such a fret of anxiety to get home, and anyway her appetite had completely deserted her over these last few days.

She tried to say something, to reassure the shadowy figure coming towards her that she was perfectly all right, but the words wouldn't come and she was spinning wildly in a black vortex of darkness that refused to let her go.

She was, she recognised in shocked surprise, despite all her claims to the contrary, about to faint.

CHAPTER TWO

'But I never faint!'

Sara frowned, recognising her own voice. She opened her eyes and discovered that she was lying in the back of a Land Rover, and moreover that there was something hard and lumpy under her spine. She tried to move, but a pair of large male hands restrained her.

'Not so fast, otherwise you'll be off again. Keep still for a moment.'

'Off again...' What on earth did he think she was? she wondered indignantly. 'I never faint,' she repeated firmly. 'And if you would just let go of me...'

She tried to sit up, to struggle against him, and gasped in shock at the way her head started to swim the moment she lifted it from the floor.

'Keep still. You'll feel better if you do.'

The deep voice, so calm, so authoritative, ought to have annoyed her, but for some reason it had exactly the opposite effect, relaxing her tense muscles, soothing both her body and her mind so that this time she stayed where she was, closing her eyes, conscious of the hard fingers circling her wrist, monitoring her pulse.

'Now try breathing slowly and deeply. Not too deeply...'

Again, half to her own astonishment, she did as she was instructed, finding it easy somehow to match her breathing to the even cadences of the voice instructing her.

'Feeling any better?'

This time, when she opened her eyes and nodded, the world didn't spin round her but stayed stationary.

'It's my own fault,' she announced as she sat up, a little more cautiously and far more successfully this time. She was, she realised, in the back of Stuart Delaney's Land Rover. It smelled of fresh, clean earth, of rain and growing things. 'I didn't have anything to eat before I left London.'

No need to tell him that she had not in fact eaten properly for several days, not merely several hours.

She winced a little as she had an unwanted mental vision of Anna's soft femininity, her curves, the fluid contours of her flesh, so much a contrast to her own more angular slenderness. Thin and dried-up, that was how Anna had dismissively described her, making her feel somehow desiccated, withered, old almost, even though Anna was in actual fact two years her senior.

Men didn't like thin women; they liked curves, softness, the ripe promise of a female body that was alluringly shaped; and she tensed a little, waiting for Stuart Delaney to make some comment about her thinness, but instead to her relief he merely commented almost absently, 'Well, we all do it at times, when we've more important things on our minds. Done it myself. In fact . . .'

She was sitting up now, ruefully conscious of the fact that the dirty interior of the Land Rover wouldn't have done her cream suit much good.

'Look, I was just on my way home. I haven't eaten myself yet. Since your parents aren't here, why don't you join me? Mrs Gibbons from the village will have been up today to give the place a clean. She normally leaves me something to eat, and in view of the hospitality I've received from your parents...'

It would be foolish to refuse his offer. This wasn't London, where a woman had to be wary of invitations and approaches from any man on such a short acquaintance. And besides, she already knew from her mother's phone calls how much her parents liked their new neighbour.

The alternative was remaining at home on her own, brooding, remembering...

'Well, if you're sure you don't mind...'

'If I minded, I wouldn't have suggested it in the first place.'

There was more than a touch of brusqueness in his comment, but instead of feeling rebuffed by it Sara found that it was refreshing almost. He was so very different from Ian. Ian, whose charm had masked a cruelty, a callousness that had left her feeling as though she had been mauled and left sore and bleeding when a harder, cleaner blow would have been kinder.

'Fine. I'll follow you up to the house in my own car, shall I?' she suggested, but Stuart Delaney shook his head.

'No, better not... I doubt that you're likely to faint again, but it's best not to take the chance.'

'Oh, but that means you'll have to bring me back,' she began to protest, but he had apparently stopped listening to her, and was walking to the rear of the Land Rover, jumping out and heading for the driver's door.

Sara started to follow him. She was no stranger to travelling in the back of beaten-up old Land Rovers, and had done so on many occasions during her teens, and so she knew from experience just how uncomfortable a ride she was likely to have if she stayed where she was. No, she would be far more comfortable in the passenger seat.

As she reached the rear of the vehicle, she slipped off her high heels and prepared to struggle down to the ground with the handicap of her straight skirt, but to her amazement Stuart, who she thought had left her to make her own way out of the Land Rover, was waiting for her, calmly scooping her up in his arms.

'Please . . . there's no need for you to do this,' she protested breathlessly, clutching her shoes with one hand and discovering very quickly that it was necessary to cling to the front of his shirt with the other.

It was very difficult to sound cool and businesslike with her head tucked into his shoulder and her fingertips inadvertently brushing the warm bare flesh of his throat.

It disconcerted her to realise how oddly aware of him she was, how very quickly and unexpectedly her breathing had altered to become shallow and quick as her body registered the proximity of his.

A look of startled bewilderment darkened her eyes, causing her to immediately close them as her body tensed against the sensations she was experiencing.

It was just the total unexpectedness of being held like this, she told herself. How long had it been since a man had picked her up and held her in his arms?

How long had it been since she had experienced this kind of male-to-female intimacy in any form at all, no matter how non-sexual?

She tried to remember, to conjure up some corresponding mental image to offset the peculiar and unwanted sensations that were causing her such discomfort and embarrassment, and could not do so.

Oh, there had been occasions in her teens... boys... clumsy, awkward kisses and embraces; but she had always been on the shy side... and then since she had met Ian...

As he felt her tension, Stuart stopped moving, and told her equably, 'It's OK, I'm not going to drop you. Don't forget I'm used to carrying half-grown trees about, and if you're thinking *they* don't need to be treated as fragile and easily damaged, then you're wrong. There is nothing more vulnerable and open to damage than a young tree removed from its habitat.

'A moment's carelessness, and the bruising and root damage which can be caused can prove fatal.'

Sara found she was battling against a half-hysterical desire to start giggling. Here she was, worrying about that startling *frisson* of physical sensation being in Stuart's arms had aroused within her, tensing herself against his answering awareness of it, only to discover that in her rescuer's eyes she was simply a sapling he was carrying from one place to another; that he was neither aware of nor

concerned about the physical intimacy of their
bodies in any sexual way at all and that he was totally oblivious to that tiny shudder of sensation that
had run through her, coiling the muscles of her
stomach, making her aware of the disconcerting
hardening of her nipples.

It had been a long time since her body had reacted
like that, she recognised, as he balanced her against
him and eased her into the passenger seat of the
Land Rover. Once, all it had needed to set her body
on fire with aching need had been for Ian to walk
into the same room; simply to hear his voice, to
register his presence had been sufficient. But just
lately... She frowned, trying to remember just when
it had last been that her body had reacted physically to his presence, to his sexuality, and
acknowledged that she could not do so. Which was
strange, surely, when she loved him...

She was still frowning when Stuart got into the
driver's seat of the vehicle and put it in motion.

'Sexless' was how Anna had tauntingly described
her, and in her heart of hearts Sara had admitted
the accuracy of the taunt. She loved Ian, and of
course she desired him, but over the years that
desire had become muted, tamed. So much so that
she had virtually forgotten what it was like to feel
that sharp, biting ache within her body, that overwhelming physical feminine responsiveness to a
man's maleness; that she had honestly believed
herself to have passed beyond the excitement of
sexuality into more mature waters.

And yet here she was reacting in exactly the way
she had thought impossible—and not to Ian...Ian,
whom she loved...but to another man, a stranger—

a man, moreover, who had given her no encouragement whatsoever to think of him in any sexual terms.

As he drove down the lane, she wondered uneasily what was happening to her, why her body had seen fit to rebel in such an unexpected and disconcerting fashion. She even began to wonder uneasily if she might have been wiser to have refused Stuart's invitation to share his supper. And then common sense reasserted itself and she reminded herself mockingly that it was hardly likely that she was going to spend the evening locked in Stuart Delaney's arms, and that, since that odd and totally unwanted sensual *frisson* of pleasure had only occurred when he had held her, she was perfectly safe from experiencing it again.

In fact, she told herself firmly, she would be better advised to put the whole incident right out of her mind. After all, her emotions had been through so many traumas recently that it was hardly surprising if she experienced the odd unexpected reaction.

As she saw the shadowy bulk of the manor house taking shape in the darkness ahead of them, she tried not to listen to the small, sharp voice that told her that her reaction to Stuart had been physical and not emotional.

After all, she knew herself well enough to feel completely secure and confident that she was not the type of woman who would ever need to seek reassurance and comfort, or even a confirmation of her desirability and femininity, in any compulsion to experience an intimacy with a man which was purely physical. After all, she reminded herself bitterly, hadn't Anna and Ian already made it devastatingly plain to her that she was not the kind of woman whom men desired or found physically attractive? She would be a fool even to think of putting that denunciation to the test . . . of trying to prove them wrong by . . .

The direction of her thoughts brought her to an abrupt and shocked halt. A physical relationship with a man who wasn't Ian? A man she did not love? Was she out of her mind? Had the shock of recent events virtually unbalanced her mentally as well as emotionally?

Stop it, she warned herself angrily. You've got enough problems to deal with without looking for more.

It had been several years since Sara had last visited the manor house—a duty visit with her mother one Christmas to the old man who used to live there—but as a child she had always found the place fascinating, and now, as Stuart brought the Land Rover to a halt at the rear of the building in what had originally been the stable yard, she turned to him and asked him impulsively, 'What made you decide to buy this place?'

He gave her a brief smile. He had a nice smile, she noticed, and an unexpected dimple on the left-hand side of his mouth. She had to subdue an odd urge to reach out and touch it. It gave him a vulnerability totally opposed to her initial impression of him as a man as tough as granite.

He might not have Ian's golden good looks, but he was a very attractive man none the less, she recognised, on a small spurt of surprise, a man a woman would feel she could depend on, trust...a man who would make a good father.

She was startled by the waywardness of her own thoughts. Where on earth were they coming from? A good father... What a ridiculous thought to have about a man she barely knew.

'It was the woodland,' she heard him saying to her, and frowned until she realised he was answering her own question. 'Not because of the quality of the trees in it. In all honesty they're pretty poor. Most of the oaks have had to come down, although I've been hoping to be able to use the wood once it's matured. No, it was because the soil here...the land, is perfect, or as near perfect as I'm likely to get for my purposes. The acreage that goes with the house is sufficient for my needs, and the land is sheltered by the Welsh hills. It's well watered but not marshy. I must admit I was worried at first about the risk of transplanting our stock up here, but so far our losses have been minimal and the new trees we've planted are doing very well. It's always risky transplanting mature trees; that's why, before we sell one, I like to check on where it's going and to make sure the buyer is aware of the maintenance programme that's necessary until it's securely rooted. Of course, with all the recent storm damage, we've done very well on the sales side, but that also puts pressure on us to produce more stock, which takes time.'

Sara was both fascinated and confused.

'I didn't think it was possible to transplant mature trees.'

'It isn't unless they've been specially grown for that purpose. My uncle started the business, seeing a gap in the market, and in the main supplying councils. When he died I inherited it from him. I was already working for the Forestry Commission. In fact I was on secondment in Canada at the time. At first I intended to sell the business, but then we had the storms of '87 which put pressure on all suppliers of mature trees—and there aren't many of us—and somehow or other I found I was hooked and that the business had grown on me, so to speak, but we needed to expand, and so I started looking for somewhere to relocate.'

'It sounds fascinating,' Sara commented, and genuinely meant it, but she could see from the sudden tightening of his mouth that he thought she was being sarcastic.

Impulsively she touched him, and said quickly, 'No, I meant it. It *does* sound fascinating. I had no idea that it was possible to transplant large trees.'

There was a small pause and then he replied, 'If you really are interested, while you're up here, I could show you round...show you what we're doing.'

'I'd like that.'

She was surprised to discover that she genuinely meant it, and not just because it would be a means of keeping Ian out of her thoughts if only for a short space of time.

'Are you feeling OK now?' he was asking her. 'Or——'

'No. No, I'm fine,' she assured him quickly. It was one thing to tell herself that that momentary and discomfiting sexual response to him meant nothing and was hardly likely to happen again. It was quite another to put that belief to the test, especially so soon after that first uncomfortably enlightening occurrence.

'So far I haven't been able to do much to the house,' he warned her as they crossed the yard, and security lights came on, illuminating the cobbles and the empty stables as well as the jumble of windows and doors that studded the weathered stone of the building.

'As I said, Mrs Gibbons comes up from the village a couple of times a week. I've managed to make the kitchen habitable, plus one of the bed-rooms, but as for the rest...'

'It's a very large house for one man,' Sara ventured.

They had almost reached the back door and he paused now, turning to look at her.

'Yes,' he agreed bleakly. 'When I bought it, I hadn't actually visualised living here alone.'

Immediately Sara guessed what must have happened. Like her, he had obviously been rejected by the person he loved. Perhaps she had not wanted to live in such an isolated spot. Perhaps she had been someone he had met in Canada who had not wanted to come and live in England, who had not loved him enough. No one knew better than she how much that kind of rejection hurt... how it scarred and wounded. She wanted to reach out to him, to touch him, to offer him her sympathy, her understanding, but he was already turning away from her, extracting some keys from his pocket and unlocking the kitchen door.

As he held it open for her, he reached inside and flicked on the lights.

Sara stepped past him and into the generous-sized room, catching her breath in admiration as she saw how it had been transformed from the dreary place she remembered.

Walls had been moved to make the room larger; the kitchen range, which she vaguely remembered as a crouching evil monster that belched smoke and was covered in rust, had been transformed somehow or other into a model of polished perfection, whose presence warmed the entire room, offering the two cats curled up on top of it a comfortable place to sleep.

Where she remembered a haphazard collection of tatty utilitarian cupboards, and a chipped stone sink, there were now beautifully made units in what she suspected was reclaimed oak, from the quality and sheen of their finish. The original stone floor had been cleaned and polished and was now partially covered with earth-toned Indian rugs; the walls had been painted a soft, warm, peachy terracotta colour; on the dresser, which like the units was oak and softly polished, stood a collection of pewter jugs and a service of traditional willow-pattern china.

A deep, comfortably solid-looking settee was pulled up close to the range, and the table in the centre of the room looked large enough and solid enough to accommodate a good-sized family.

In fact all that the room lacked to make it perfect was perhaps some flowers in the heavy pewter jugs, and of course the delicious warm smell of food cooking which she always associated with her mother's kitchen and her mother's love.

'This is wonderful,' she commented admiringly, swinging round to face Stuart and to say wryly, 'I don't know who installed these units for you, but I do know that they must have cost the earth—the quality of the wood alone...'

'Reclaimed oak,' he told her offhandedly. 'I picked it up quite cheaply, and as for the units...' He shrugged, and turned away from her.

'I made them myself. Not a particularly difficult task.'

He sounded so offhand that for a moment Sara felt embarrassed that she had enthused about them so much, and then she recognised that her praise had probably embarrassed him, that he perhaps wasn't actually used to his talents being admired.

While she assimilated these thoughts, she chalked up another black mark against the woman who had rejected him. Had he built this kitchen for her, working on it with love and hope, only to find...?

Tears stung her eyes. She blinked them away hurriedly, and heard herself saying in an oddly choked voice, 'Well, no matter what you say, *I* think they look wonderful. The wood—there's something about it that makes you want to touch it...to stroke it almost...' She broke off, feeling thoroughly embarrassed as she realised that he had turned round and was scrutinising her.

'Not many people recognise that quality in wood, that appeal; to most of them it's simply...wood. They don't recognise its tactile appeal...' He stopped. 'Sorry, I'm starting to lecture you. If you haven't eaten all day you must be starving. I'll see what Mrs G. has left.'

He opened the door and disappeared in the direction of what Sara remembered as being one of the house's cold pantries, returning within seconds with a covered dish.

'It looks like shepherd's pie,' he told her.

'Wonderful.' She could feel her empty stomach starting to grumble hungrily at the thought of food.

This was the first time she had actually felt hungry since Ian had dropped the bombshell announcement of his engagement. The first time she had found herself able to forget her own problems and become interested in something and someone else, she recognised as Stuart switched on the oven and opened it, placing the pie dish on one of its runners.

'Mrs G. tells me that it is possible to cook things in the range,' he told Sara ruefully. 'But as yet I haven't quite mastered the knack.'

'I'm not surprised.'

Sara told him about her visits to the house as a child, admiring the way he had managed to restore the range.

'I enjoyed it. In the winter, when the daylight hours are so short, having the house to work on is an ideal means of finding something to do.'

He paused, his face slightly shadowed, and Sara wondered sympathetically if he was thinking about *her*, the woman he loved . . . thinking about how different things might have been were she here to share his life with him. He looked so sombre that she half turned away from him, instinctively wanting to give him privacy for his feelings, and she was surprised to hear him saying, 'The problem is that, instead of renovating the house, what I ought to be doing is tackling the mountain of paperwork that's amassing in the study.

'That's proving to be my biggest headache since I inherited the business. It seems that an inability to deal accurately and efficiently with paperwork is a family trait. My uncle's affairs were in such a mess that I had to hire a firm of accountants to get them straightened out. They recommended a computer and a software program, both for the financial aspects of the business and for keeping a record of the replanting schemes I intend to set up, but the first time I tried to use the damn thing...' He sounded so exasperated that Sara turned to look at him. He had pushed his fingers into his hair as he spoke to her in a gesture of impatient irritation which confirmed her earlier opinion that it needed cutting.

His hair was thick and glossy, almost black, so very different from Ian's expertly styled blond hair.

'I don't know why it is, but I seem to have a blind spot where paperwork is concerned.' He was scowling slightly, suddenly looking very much younger... almost like a little boy. The thought of anyone considering such a large and tough-looking man as a little boy amused Sara enough to make a small smile curve her mouth. She saw Stuart looking at her, and realised that *he* was focusing on *her* face... on her mouth itself.

The instant reaction that ricocheted through her body stunned her into immobility, followed by an astonishing urge to touch her tongue-tip to her lips to relieve their unfamiliar dryness. It was so long since she had been aware of how very erotic it could be to have a man's attention focused on her mouth in that particular way that it was several seconds before she recognised her reaction for what it was.

Immediately her face became suffused with a wave of hot colour, which intensified as she realised abruptly that Stuart probably hadn't been focusing on her mouth in any remotely sensual way at all, but had far more likely mistaken her smile for contempt at his inability to cope with his paperwork.

Embarrassment and a desire to rectify matters rushed her into ill-considered speech, so that before she knew it she was saying quickly, 'Well, if there's anything *I* can do to help... I'm going to be here for... for some time. I might not be familiar with your software, but I could perhaps make some headway with the ordinary paperwork.'

He was watching her with so much surprise that she stopped speaking, her face burning again.

'I'm sorry,' she started to apologise. 'You've probably made arrangements of your own. You——'

'No. No, I haven't,' he assured her. 'And if you *really* mean it... I can't tell you what a headache it's been. I just don't seem to be able to get to grips with it at all. You're intending to be around for some time, then?'

'Er—yes...' She fidgeted with the buttons on her suit-jacket, biting her lip.

'As a matter of fact...' She couldn't bring herself to look at him, but sooner or later everyone locally was bound to know anyway that she had given up her London job.

'I've... I've decided to take a brief sabbatical. Spend a few months at home. I...I miss the country and my family.'

She was struggling for an explanation that would sound acceptable, logical, mature...and not the impulse decision of a child.

To her relief he didn't question her, but said instead, 'I don't blame you. London, or any other city, has never appealed to me.'

While he talked to her, Stuart was moving easily round the kitchen, taking knives and forks from a drawer, putting two of the plates to warm.

For such a big man he moved very deftly, quietly and calmly in a way that was somehow like his very presence, soothing and reassuring.

When the oven timer pinged to announce that their supper was ready, he served it up on to the two plates and handed Sara hers, suggesting that she should sit with her back to the range in order to keep warm.

'I'm afraid I'm not exactly fit to sit down and eat with someone,' he apologised ruefully as he took his own place.

He had discarded his Wellingtons when he'd come into the kitchen and had washed the mud off his hands, but he was still wearing the worn shirt and ripped jeans he had had on when they first met. However, now, instead of contrasting them with Ian's immaculate pin-striped suits and perfectly laundered shirts, Sara discovered that she actually felt more comfortable with him because he was so casually dressed. It made her feel at ease in a way she had never done with Ian...more able to relax and be herself instead of being crippled by the necessity of looking and being her best. She was, she discovered as she tucked into her food, enjoying being the recipient of his concern and attention, instead of having to do all the work...instead of having, as she had always felt she had to when she was with Ian, to do all the entertaining.

It was only as she ate that she recognised how artificial even her working relationship with Ian had been, and how she had always been striving to attain a standard of perfection which would somehow or other change his attitude towards her, make him turn to her...make him want her. She had been like someone bewitched, someone pursuing an impossible goal, she recognised uncomfortably, and yet she loved Ian; that should have meant that he of all people was the one she had felt most at home, most comfortable, most happy with.

She pushed such disturbing and unwanted thoughts aside, concentrating instead on drawing Stuart out about his plans for his business and the house.

He had a fascinating fund of stories about his years abroad working for the Forestry Commission in a variety of locations, she discovered, and their supper had long been eaten, their coffee drunk and everything washed up and cleared away, before she happened to glance at her watch and discover that it was almost one o'clock in the morning.

'Heavens, what must you think of me?' she apologised. 'Talk about guests overstaying their welcome! And I expect you'll have to be up early in the morning.'

'Not that early. Besides, it isn't often that I have the pleasure of an attractive and intelligent woman's company.'

Sara froze. Intelligent she might be...but attractive...

'Have I said something wrong?'

The quiet question threw her a little. She was so used to Ian's sometimes almost sadistic method of extending a compliment, only to withdraw it when she reached out to grasp it, that she had no idea how to react to a man who genuinely seemed not to understand that she was well aware of her lack of sexual desirability, and knew quite well that he could not possibly have found her attractive. Even so, there was no doubt that he had meant the compliment as a kindness rather than a cruelty, and she had no wish to spoil the harmony of the evening they had shared by pointing out to him that it was unnecessary for him to flatter her with remarks she knew were not true.

'I'm just rather tired,' she fibbed. 'I really ought to be making a move.'

'Yes. It *is* getting late. I'm afraid I've selfishly kept you here longer than I should. I'll drive you back now.' He paused, and seemed to consider something before asking her, 'You'll feel quite happy about staying in the house on your own?'

His thoughtfulness surprised her. She was so used to Ian's expecting her to be self-sufficient that she found it oddly heart-warming to be treated as though she were vulnerable... fragile almost.

'I'll be fine,' she assured him, adding apologetically as she remembered something she ought to have said earlier, 'I feel very guilty about the way I've taken up your evening and eaten half of your supper. So stupid of me to faint like that. I...'

'You never faint,' he broke in, grinning at her. 'Yes, I know. That was the first thing you said to me when you came round, as I remember.'

'So stupid of me...rushing down here without stopping to eat and without phoning to check that Mum and Dad would be here. I must ring them in the morning. See how Jacqui's getting on.'

'It was a spur-of-the-moment decision to leave London and...and your job, then?' Stuart asked her a few minutes later as they walked towards the Land Rover.

She knew that in the circumstances it was a natural enough question, but even so she could feel herself tensing, her skin tight with discomfort and despair, her heart aching as she dwelt on exactly why she had come home so precipitately, like a child running back to the comfort of its parents' arms.

'In a way...'

Something in her response must have warned him off, because he said, far more formally, 'I'm sorry. I didn't mean to pry.'

'No, that's all right.' She was, she realised, probably over-reacting, and besides...besides, suddenly, for some reason she couldn't really fathom, she wanted to tell him the truth. She had always loathed pretence, deceit...

'I gave up my job because...' She turned away from him and told him quickly, tersely, 'Because I'm in love with Ian, my boss. He doesn't love me. He never will. In fact, he's just become engaged to someone else.'

She couldn't bear to look at him.

'Pathetic, isn't it? A grown woman running home to her parents?'

'Not at all. At times of emotional trauma, I think turning to those who love us and whom we know will offer us comfort is a natural instinct we all share and possess.

'This man... Your boss... I take it there's no chance that he might change his mind...'

Sara turned to look at him, searching his face for signs of pity, but instead all she could find was compassion and sympathy.

It made her relax enough to shake her head and tell him simply, 'I fell in love with him when I was nineteen years old. Like a fool I went on hoping, believing that by some miraculous means one day he was going to turn round and look at me and somehow or other realise that he loved me. I've been a complete and utter fool, as I now know.'

She took a deep breath, suddenly determined to hold nothing back, to let him know just how much of a fool she had been. The darkness cloaking them gave her the courage she needed. There was something about him, about the sympathetic quality of his listening silence, that made it easy for her to talk to him, to confide in him. Because he was a stranger?

Perhaps... but what did it matter? Suddenly she needed to talk to someone, to tell someone, to verbalise her pain, her sense of rejection and humiliation, no matter how much she might regret doing so later.

'When his fiancée told me that they were both aware of my feelings for him, feelings which I stupidly thought I'd managed to keep secret, I knew that I couldn't go on working for him any longer.' Her mouth compressed as she remembered just what Anna had said to her.

'It was bad enough knowing that I loved him and that he would never love me. Carrying the added burden, the added humiliation of knowing that both he and Anna knew how I felt . . . knew and found it amusing . . .' She shrugged in the darkness. 'Perhaps I made the decision to leave for all the wrong reasons, but I know the decision itself was right.' She paused and then found she was unable to look at him as she added shakily, 'I don't know why I'm boring you with all of this. You must think me the world's worst fool.'

'*You're* not the fool,' Stuart told her mysteriously, his voice unexpectedly rough. 'And I do sympathise. Loving someone when you know that love can never be returned is a heavy burden to bear.'

Was he speaking from personal experience? Sara rather suspected so. Knowing that made her feel more relaxed, less self-conscious and embarrassed about the uncharacteristic way in which she had poured out her feelings to him.

'I don't know why I'm telling you all this. Normally I never——'

'Perhaps that's why. Those of us who find it difficult to confide in people close to us sometimes need the catharsis of unburdening ourselves to a stranger. You need have no fear that what you've told me will go any further.'

'Oh, no. . . I never thought that.' Sara bit her lip, horrified that he might think she would believe him capable of betraying her confidences to someone else, and at the same time conscious that her feeling of concern at having confided in him was caused by her unexpected desire for him to think well of her.

Why on earth should it matter what he thought of her? They were strangers. All right, so he might be a neighbour of her parents, but once this sabbatical of hers was over she doubted if she was likely to see him more than briefly again, so what did it matter what he thought of her, as a person or as a woman?

A small, uncomfortable *frisson* burned her skin. How could he think of her as a woman other than as Ian and Anna thought of her: as someone so sexless, so undesirable, so much a failure in the sexual aspects of her femininity that she was the butt of their jokes... their amusement?

She shivered a little, unconsciously moving slightly away from him. He was, she saw, frowning slightly as though something had annoyed him.

'So,' he commented abruptly, 'you've come home to nurse a bruised heart.'

A *bruised* heart?

'If it helps at all, it sounds to me as though *you've* had a lucky escape. Any man who could...' He broke off, while Sara stared at him. A lucky *escape*. How could he make that judgement on so little information? He knew nothing of Ian, of the manner of man he was. Was he just being kind... tactful? She searched his face, but could read nothing in the shadows cloaking his expression. He was, she realised, a man who could keep his thoughts completely to himself when he wished to do so. There was now a sternness about his expression that made her body tense a little.

'It isn't Ian's fault,' she defended. 'I should have realised years ago that...' She stopped. 'I'm sorry. You can't possibly want to hear all this. I'd better go home before I really start wallowing in self-pity...' She turned quickly away from him, suddenly feeling very self-conscious and embarrassed.

Her face was burning with hot colour as she wondered what on earth had possessed her to unburden herself to him like that.

What on earth must he be thinking of her, a woman who told him the most intimate details of her life on so short an acquaintanceship?

As though he knew what she was thinking he said abruptly, 'I admire you for telling me. It can't have been easy. It's very rare to find a woman who's willing to be so honest.'

His comment startled her into looking at him. Had *she* been deceitful, the woman who had hurt him; had she perhaps lied to him, cheated on him, or had she simply deceived him by allowing him to believe she loved him when she did not? What had she been like? Where was she now? Did he still love her... want her? Lie awake at night aching for her?

Her eyes widened as she realised how intrusive her thoughts were. She looked away from him, half afraid he might see what she was thinking.

'And, while you're staying here, if there's anything I can do to help...'

She tensed, feeling such a deep emotional response to his kindness that she could feel the tears clogging her throat. Why *was* he being so kind to her? They were strangers... Fellow feeling? Because he too had suffered what she was suffering...or was he just by nature one of those human beings with the rare gift of wanting to reach out and help others?

'I—that's very kind of you. I feel such a fool, telling you all this.'

'Please don't. There's no need.'

His words comforted her, reassured her, banishing her embarrassment, making her feel more relaxed and at ease.

Ten minutes later, as he drove her home, sitting silently beside her, she wondered where his thoughts were, and Sara wondered if he was thinking about the woman he loved, the one he would have *preferred* to have seated beside him.

She discovered an hour later, when she was finally tucked up in her childhood bedroom, that she felt envious of that unknown woman. Hadn't she re-alised how fortunate she was to be loved by a man like Stuart Delaney? A man who possessed such a quiet, supportive male strength, a man who, while he might not possess the charm of someone like Ian, nevertheless had many qualities which any sane woman would find very, very attractive. He would be a loyal and a loving husband, a good father...a true friend and partner. He would also, Sara recognised with a sudden and rather shocking pulse of sensation within her body, be a good lover...a very good lover: tender, considerate, passionate, giving...

Strange that she should know that almost automatically about Stuart and yet when it came to Ian, whom she had known for so many years, whom she had loved for so many years, when it came to trying to imagine herself describing Ian as a good lover, she discovered that her brain would not allow her to formulate the lie. Ian... She closed her eyes, trying to blot out his image, trying not to relive the cruel things Anna had said to her...trying not to imagine the two of them together, laughing about her, about her stupidity, her inadequacy...her utter lack of desirability.

CHAPTER THREE

AMAZINGLY, Sara slept better than she had done in a long time, even before the trauma of the recent events in her life.

When she woke up and discovered that it was gone eight o'clock, she thought at first that the alarm must be wrong, and then put her deep and refreshing sleep down to the change of air.

It was only when she was downstairs, enjoying the mug of richly fragrant coffee that she had just made for herself, that she wondered if the evening she had spent with Stuart Delaney might have had some bearing on her deep and dreamless sleep.

Stuart Delaney.

She put down her mug and frowned a little. Last night he had been so kind, so compassionate, but she knew that if it hadn't been for her idiocy in fainting she would never have allowed him to get close enough to her to reveal those characteristics. In fact, when she really thought about it, she was forced to admit that in the years when her love for Ian had obsessed and possessed her to the exclusion of anything else she had quite deliberately set up mental and emotional barriers within herself which had kept other people at bay. Other *people*. *Not* just other men... Because she had known deep down within herself that her true friends, those with her interests at heart, those who cared for her and were concerned for her, would have tried to

persuade her not to focus her whole life on Ian—
a man who quite patently did not return her
feelings—but instead to try to make friendships,
relationships with other people.

Had she deliberately taken the line that the fewer
people who knew about her feelings for Ian, the
fewer people she admitted to her life, the less chance
there was of anyone trying to dissuade her from
what she was doing... wasting her life?

Wasting her life? She worried at her bottom lip.
Was that what she was doing? Had all those years
of loving Ian, of waiting, wanting, hoping, been
nothing more than a waste?

Only if she was not prepared to learn from them,
to acknowledge the self-destructiveness of what she
had done and to prevent herself from ever re-
peating the same folly again.

And that meant starting right now. From today,
from this moment she was going to focus on the
present... on the future... and not on the past.

She had accepted now that Ian would never love
her; that there would never have come a day, even
without Anna, when he would have looked at her,
when that special dazzling smile of his, the one that
unfailingly made her heart turn over and her
muscles go weak, would be tinged, deepened, with
an extra-special warmth; an extra-special meaning.

She felt her eyes beginning to burn, her heart
starting to pound in the familiar onset of misery
and grief.

Crying wouldn't help... giving way to her
emotions, her pain; in the end they would do her
no good whatsoever. She had come home to escape
from Ian, from her memories, not to bring them

with her...not to dwell on them...not to give in to the self-destructive urge of wallowing in self-pity and misery.

Thank goodness she had accepted Stuart Delaney's offer to visit, to spend some time looking over his new venture, she reflected as she finished her coffee. She knew next to nothing about growing trees, other than the fact that at one time investing in woodlands had been a popular tax shelter favoured by enterprising businessmen.

Stuart Delaney's venture, though, was not of that ilk. Last night, listening to him talking about the need to halt the spread of a form of reafforestation which he considered alien to a good many parts of Great Britain, and instead to replant with carefully selected, native broad-leaved varieties, she had realised that this venture was for him not simply a means of earning a living but something that meant a great deal to him in emotional terms as well.

Her frown deepened slightly. She was surprised to discover how much she was looking forward to seeing Stuart Delaney again. He had been so easy to get on with. Time had passed so quickly.

Should she simply drive up there, or should she telephone him first? They hadn't specified a time for her to meet him last night.

She would, she decided, simply have to drive over there, since she did not have his telephone number, but first there was something she had to do.

As she picked up the telephone receiver and dialled the number of her sister's home, she wondered anxiously how her sister, and her new baby, if it had now been born, were doing.

Her mother answered the telephone, saying immediately, 'Sara... I was just beginning to get worried about you. I rang you half a dozen times or so at home, and then I rang Ian's office. When there was no reply from either number... Where are you? What——?'

'I'm at home, Mum. I arrived last night. I should have rung you first, but... Anyway, luckily for me, your new neighbour just happened to be driving past and he explained to me that you'd had a call from David and that you'd had to drop everything and rush over there. How is Jacqui? The baby?'

'Jacqui is fine; a bit shell-shocked, I think. After all, she still had over a month to go. The baby is fine as well. A little girl, so you can imagine how thrilled she and David are after the two boys.'

'They've decided to call her Jessica. The hospital are keeping them both in for a few days, just as a precaution, so your father and I will be staying on down here for at least another week.'

Another week. Sara gnawed at her mouth, wincing a little as she realised how much she had been maltreating it recently. It felt swollen and sore, the flesh bruised and sensitive.

'Do you mind if I stay on here until you get back?'

'Of course not,' her mother assured her. 'It is still your home, darling, you know that. Have you some holidays to use up?' She paused and then asked more worriedly, with maternal anxiety, 'Sara, you aren't ill?'

'Everything's fine,' she fibbed firmly. There would be time enough to tell her parents about her decision to give up her job with Ian once they returned home. Although it was a subject they had never discussed, she suspected that her mother at least might have guessed how she felt about Ian, and she had an idea that she would be pleased she had made the decision to break away from him, especially once she had explained that he was getting married.

Anna and her cruel revelations were not subjects she could or wanted to discuss with her family; that was after all one of the reasons she had come here in the first place, to escape from the curious questions of her friends, from their well-meaning but painful attempts to discover what had happened and why she had handed in her notice.

She had barely replaced the receiver, having spoken to both her excited nephews about the birth of their new sister, and to her brother-in-law, who sounded almost as incoherent and thrilled as his sons, when the telephone rang.

She answered it automatically, assuming it would be someone wanting her parents, but to her surprise it was Stuart Delaney on the other end of the line.

'I just remembered,' he told her, 'that we didn't arrange a time to meet last night. I have to go into the village, and I was going to suggest that I picked you up on the way back if that's convenient.'

About to protest that there was no reason for him to do that and that she could quite easily drive herself up to the manor, Sara recognised that it was silly to use two cars when he was passing the house anyway, swallowed her instinctive desire to prove that she was independent and quite capable of looking after herself, and said instead, 'Well, if you're sure you don't mind...'

'If I did, I wouldn't have suggested it.'

His response startled her a little. She still wasn't used to such bluntness. Ian would never have been so forthright. Ian...Ian... She felt her throat start to close up and swallowed hard, clinging to the deep, slightly rough texture of Stuart Delaney's voice as he told her what time he would be picking her up.

'I'm looking forward to it,' she told him politely when he had finished speaking.

'So am I.'

For some reason, the simple comment set off the most extraordinary reaction inside her.

A fluttery, heady, expansive feeling of antici-pation and excitement immediately followed by a sharper, warning sense of danger and fear.

What was she frightened of, for heaven's sake— what was there to fear? Not Stuart Delaney, surely? She couldn't remember the last time she had felt so at ease with anyone. Perhaps that was it, she reflected a few minutes later as she replaced the receiver; perhaps it was the very fact that she *did* feel so at ease with him that made her feel appre-hensive. In her present vulnerable state, the last thing she needed to do was to become emotionally involved with another man.

Emotionally *involved*? With Stuart Delaney? A man who after all had been a stranger to her until last night? Ridiculous. Impossible. After all, how *could* she be in any danger of becoming emotionally involved, emotionally dependent on another man when she still loved Ian?

She was being silly, over-cautious, looking for problems that could not possibly exist.

No, she had nothing to fear from Stuart Delaney. He, like her, had suffered the agony of loving the wrong person, and just like her he would be anxious to avoid an emotional relationship. She wondered how long it had been since his romance had broken up. He was a very attractive man; not good-looking in the way that Ian was good-looking, of course, but very attractive none the less, if one liked the rugged outdoors type, and many women did.

Had he remained celibate since the end of his relationship? Such things were harder for men, so one was led to believe. Of course she and Ian had never been lovers. No man had *ever* been her lover, she reflected a little savagely.

She had not minded that, not while she was still forcing herself to believe her delusion that one day Ian was going to look at her and want her...love her. But now that she had been forced to face up to the truth...

She was twenty-nine years old...a twenty-nine-year-old virgin. She smiled wryly to herself. What *was* she saying? That she regretted the fact that she had not at some period of her life experienced the intimacy of sharing her body with a lover? If so, was that so very wrong? She was forced to accept that mentally and emotionally it would be harder for her now at twenty-nine, with the added maturity that a decade brought, to actively contemplate a purely physical affair; that her awareness, not just of the changing social climate, which had led to a far less promiscuous and more cautious outlook on casual sex, but also of herself as a woman, of her inhibition and reserve, which told her that she could never be the kind of woman who would find it easy to share an intimate relationship with a man to whom she was not deeply emotionally, and mentally committed would make it impossible.

Harder? She smiled grimly to herself. Why not face the truth? It would be impossible. Which meant... which meant that unless she was prepared to take Margaret's advice and look for a pleasant, like-minded man, with whom she could settle down, she was unlikely to have the opportunity to have the family, the children she knew she wanted.

Not for her the brief casual affair, resulting in a pregnancy and a child that would be hers and hers alone. And as for falling in love... Well, that wasn't going to happen either, was it? She had fallen in love with Ian and look what that had led to.

Even if she could ever manage to stop loving him...

She sighed faintly to herself. These were morbid, unwise thoughts. She would be better employed in turning her mind to other, less emotive topics.

She wondered if Stuart Delaney had found a way of coming to terms with his emotional pain and, if so, if he perhaps had any tips he could pass on to her.

Surprisingly, for someone who had always guarded her privacy so intensely, and who had never easily made friends with members of the opposite sex, she found that she could contemplate the idea of discussing her situation with Stuart Delaney with astonishing ease.

Perhaps because so many of her barriers had already been down at the moment of their initial meeting, she felt as though she had known him far longer and far more intimately than a mere handful of hours.

She was, she discovered, as she glanced at her watch to check the time, actually looking forward to seeing him, actually aware of a quite distinct tremor of excitement and anticipation running through her body as she listened for the sound of his arrival.

When Stuart arrived a few minutes earlier than he had said she was taken a little by surprise. Ian was never early for anything, and was in fact invariably late, salving the offence with one of his charming, apologetic smiles, and yet somehow always leaving one with the feeling of being not quite important enough to have merited the compliment of his arriving on time. As she picked up her jacket and bag, she wondered a little bitterly if he ever kept Anna waiting.

Somehow she doubted it. Anna had not struck her as the type of woman who would wait for any man.

It was only as she was locking the door behind her that she realised that she was actually thinking how well suited the pair of them were in their selfishness. The thought was enough to make her stand still where she was, her body frozen in shock as she contemplated the almost heretical nature of her own thoughts. Never in all the years she had worked for him and loved him had she ever allowed herself to criticise Ian even in the deepest privacy of her own thoughts, her own often very sore heart, and yet now here she was doing so, and finding it shockingly easy.

Uneasily she realised that had she not loved Ian so deeply she might almost have disliked him...despised him. Take away the blinkering effect of his intense good looks, take away the charm—which she was beginning to realise was no more than surface deep—and what were you left with? A very selfish self-absorbed man with a nature, a personality that repelled rather than attracted her.

It was an unpleasant discovery. She had never considered herself to be silly enough to place any undue importance on a person's looks. Their personality, their warmth, their responsiveness to others—these were what mattered, and yet here she was admitting that had Ian *not* been so good-looking... And it was no excuse reminding herself that she had only been a very impressionable nineteen when she met him. She wasn't nineteen any longer.

'Something wrong?'

The concern in Stuart's voice as he opened the gate and came up the path made her shake her head.

'Thank goodness. I thought for a moment there might have been bad news.'

Bad news? From Ian, did he mean?

When she looked puzzled, he explained, 'From your mother...your sister.'

Instantly Sara's face flooded with guilty colour. 'Oh, no. Mother and baby—a little girl—are both doing fine, although Mum and Dad will be staying on for a little while. Actually I must drive into Ludlow tomorrow and get a card, and something for the baby. They're going to call her Jessica.'

'Nice,' Stuart approved. 'Is David pleased?'

'Over the moon. He's been longing for a daughter.'

'A wise man. I must admit I've always had a yen for a couple of pigtailed serious-eyed daughters myself. Not that I've anything against sons. In fact . . .' He gave her a wry glance. 'It doesn't just seem to be your sex that suffer the urge to reproduce the species once they get to their thirties. Men suffer a similar syndrome.'

Sara looked at him in some surprise.

'You want children?'

Ian, who was in his early thirties, had been very voluble in his belief that children were a nuisance, a hindrance to the kind of life he personally wanted to lead, and somehow or other she had supposed that the majority of unmarried men in their thirties must feel the same way.

'Very much; don't you?'

The directness of his answer and the question that followed it shook her a little bit. No matter how comfortable she felt with him, she was still surprised by his straightforwardness.

'Yes . . . yes, I do,' she admitted a little hesitantly. 'In fact . . .' She paused, and then reminded herself that there was no need for her to conceal her true thoughts from Stuart as there had been from Ian.

'In fact, just before I left London, my next-door neighbour, a close friend, was suggesting that I ought to consider finding someone to marry who shared my love of children. She claims that that's what she did. That she heard her biological clock ticking away extremely loudly and extremely fast, and that when she met Ben, and discovered they had a great deal in common, she married him, knowing he would be a good father for their children, rather than because she was in love with him. In her case it all worked out very well, since she does now love him very much.'

'Mmm. On the face of it, and using today's mores and standards, it does seem a cold-blooded arrangement, and yet it isn't really so very many generations ago that marriages were arranged either by one's parents, or other family relatives, for reasons that had very little to do with the emotional needs of the parties concerned, and on the face of it those relationships worked.'

'Probably because people's choices were so much more limited. Divorce wasn't possible and so they had to stay together, and, of course, then in every stratum of society the time that husbands and wives actually spent together was far more limited than it is today. Families played a much larger role in people's lives than they do now. Newly married couples had the support and advice of not just parents and siblings to call on, but a vast clan of aunts, uncles, cousins and more.'

'Yes, that's true. I take it you don't consider your friend's advice worth taking?'

Sara paused as she reached his Land Rover.

'In one sense, yes. In others...' She gave a tiny shrug. 'I *do* want children...very much, I always have done. But to marry a man I don't love...'

'There are many differing degrees of love,' Stuart surprised her by saying. 'Perhaps it sounds cynical, but I suspect that the securest and most enduring foundation for a stable relationship between a man and a woman isn't necessarily based on the euphoric and very often totally unrealistic state we describe as "being in love".

'Mutual understanding: mutual goals, respect, leavened by a shared sense of humour, will in my estimation take a relationship a good deal further.'

Sara was shocked enough to protest. 'But what about desire? Surely...'

He was standing close enough to her for her to see the way the tawny gold of his eyes suddenly became darkly brilliant. An unfamiliar *frisson* of sensation twisted through her and her skin suddenly burned with heated colour as she reacted to him with a mixture of embarrassment and shock.

What on earth was she doing raising such a topic with a man she barely knew? It wasn't, after all, a subject she would even have raised with Ian. In fact, it was a subject it would have been impossible to raise with Ian.

'It is possible to experience desire without love, of course, but using that kind of physical need as something on which to base a permanent relationship isn't something I personally would ever contemplate. Nevertheless, there has, I agree, to be desire, but desire like love itself takes many shapes and forms. And what is desire? A couple for whom sex is the most important part of their relationship would say that sex is desire, but there are other couples who, although they might not admit it, are more strongly motivated by a desire for money, a desire for social position, even a desire for children, and these desires are the most important focus of their relationships.

'For me a marriage founded on mutual goals, mutual trust and respect, a mutual willingness to make the relationship work, plus a mutual desire to have children, are more important than intensely powerful sex, no matter how alluring that particular desire might sometimes seem.'

'If you want children so much, why...?'

Sara stopped. How on earth could she have forgotten so quickly that Stuart, like her, had lost the person he loved?

'Why haven't I married?' he finished for her, tactfully easing her embarrassment. 'Probably because I haven't found the right woman. It isn't easy being married to a man with a job like mine. It's demanding work, involving long hours, and limited financial reward. The trees need constant attention even when one has an experienced and well-trained staff. Holidays, that sort of thing, are a luxury I simply can't afford, and it takes a very special kind of woman to accept the limitations my work would place on our ability for personal freedom.

'One of the reasons I relocated out here was because, apart from anything else, the old site was in an area which had slowly become more and more urbanised, and finding staff was growing increasingly difficult.

'Boys who were quite willing to work outdoors in the summer when the weather was good were not quite so happy about outdoor work in the winter. Moving to a farming community where it would be easier to find people prepared to take on outdoor work seemed a sensible idea.'

He smiled at her as he handed her up into the Land Rover and then closed the door. When he had walked round to the driver's door, climbed in and set the vehicle in motion, he continued, 'It isn't just the care and maintenance of the trees while we're growing them, which is difficult enough. They have to be grown in such a way that, when necessary, we can lift them with a good solid root-ball. Not easy when you're talking about a half-grown tree which might in maturity reach eighty feet and weigh a couple of tons. There's also the problem of supplying adequate after-sales care, to ensure that the newly transplanted tree doesn't die. I've lost a couple through poor care on the part of the new owners, and I can tell you there's nothing more soul-destroying. I hate to see a healthy tree die out of sheer ignorance and neglect, especially when I know it's a tree that ought to have survived and flourished.'

The emotion he was feeling was deepening his voice, making it slightly harsh and abrasive. He really loved his trees, Sara recognised, and if he felt like that about them then she couldn't help reflecting what a wonderfully caring father he would be.

It was amazingly easy to picture him mentally with his two little girls and his sons as well, a happy smiling woman by his side, she acknowledged wistfully. Why on earth had she rejected him, the woman he had loved? If *she* were loved by a man like Stuart...

A man like Stuart? But she loved *Ian*, who was as different as it was possible to be from Stuart.

This was ridiculous, she chided herself, as Stuart changed gear and turned into the manor's drive. She was obviously suffering from some kind of reaction to the trauma of the last few days, seeing in Stuart all the virtues she now realised that Ian did not possess.

Seeing his virtues was one thing, she derided herself, but picturing him as the father of four children was quite another.

'I haven't got round to using the main entrance to the house as yet,' Stuart told her apologetically as he brought the Land Rover to a halt in the cobbled yard.

'In fact, as far as the house is concerned, I'm afraid I just haven't had the time to do a great deal with it. I bought the place because of the land— the house was an ancillary feature, and I have to admit I didn't even look round it properly. I didn't realise until I moved in how large it is.'

'Well, it certainly has the potential to hold a large family,' Sara murmured, adding mischievously, 'A very large family.'

He turned in his seat and looked at her.

'Indeed it does,' he agreed wryly. 'It's large enough for a veritable tribe of offspring.'

They both laughed, and as they did Sara realised how impossible it would have been for her to have shared this moment with Ian. His sense of humour was sharp and cutting, malicious sometimes, and confined to the foibles and vulnerabilities of people he knew combined with how they measured up to his own very individualistic table of good and bad points, a table which seemed to be largely comprised of media and social 'in' jokes and rules.

'By the way,' Stuart asked her, 'I was wondering. Would you still be willing to cast your expert eye over the havoc I've created with my paperwork? You did say...'

'No problem. I'd be only too glad to,' Sara assured him. 'It will give me something to keep me occupied while I wait for Mum and Dad to come home.'

'Well, it will take quite a while to show you over what we're doing here. I was hoping I might be able to persuade you to stay for lunch. Not one of Mrs G.'s offerings this time. I bought some stuff while I was out this morning. I don't know if you like fresh salmon.'

'I love it,' Sara assured him. 'And I'd also love to see over the house. If you don't think it's too intrusive of me to ask.'

'Not at all,' Stuart assured her. 'Although I warn you it isn't exactly *Homes and Gardens*.'

Sara laughed. 'Good,' she told him with a smile. 'Other people's perfection always makes me feel dreadfully inferior.'

'Yes, I know what you mean,' Stuart agreed, as he opened his door. She made to do the same, but he stopped her.

'Hang on,' he said. 'It's quite a long way down out of this thing. I'll come round and give you a hand.'

Sara could have told him that she'd been scrambling out of Land Rovers since she was no higher than her father's knee, but for some reason she refrained.

There was something undeniably pleasant, after Anna's scathing and cruel remarks about her lack of sexuality, her lack of femininity, in having a man perform the small courtesy of helping her out of his vehicle even though it might be unnecessary.

It made her feel fragile, and delicate, all the things she knew quite well she wasn't and never had been. It made her feel that she was a woman, she recognised in startled comprehension, something that Ian hadn't done in a long time, and something she hadn't allowed any other man to do, because of Ian.

And so she waited, with her door closed, smiling at Stuart as he opened it for her, releasing her seatbelt, so that she could start to climb out of the Land Rover.

She had assumed that Stuart would simply give her a guiding hand, an arm to lean on if necessary as she stepped down on to the ground, and was therefore startled when instead he reached into the Land Rover and placed his hands firmly on her waist.

As he leaned towards her, their eyes were virtually on the same level. His were a dark warm gold, flecked with tawny highlights. They were very masculine eyes, she acknowledged, despite the length and thickness of those dark lashes. They were also very perceptive eyes; eyes that seemed to recognise her momentary shock at the sensation of his hands against her body, warming her flesh through her jeans and shirt, making her suddenly almost painfully aware of the fact that virtually the only physical contact her body had had with that of a man had been limited to the clumsy caresses of her teenage years; that there had never been a time when a man had held her like this as a preamble to a more intimate embrace; that she had never in fact experienced the sensual tension that came from knowing that the male hands resting on her waist would soon be sliding upwards over her ribcage to caress her breasts, that the dark male head so close to her own would soon be obliterating the light as they shared the intimacy of a lovers' kiss.

A lovers' kiss. Unable to stop herself, she looked at Stuart's mouth. Her heart was thudding frantically, her breathing jerky and unsteady.

An embarrassing sensual awareness of him as a man seemed to rocket through her, totally throwing her off guard. She started to tremble, to shiver as her body was gripped with an unfamiliar tension, a sharp aching need that seemed to burst into life inside her, taking over her entire nervous system so quickly that she was given no chance to control it. She closed her eyes, feeling sick with shock and self-disgust.

'Sara... Are you all right?'

Her eyes opened automatically, focusing on Stuart.

'I... I...'

'You're trembling.'

He said it almost accusingly, his grip on her waist tightening.

What on earth could she say? How on earth could she explain? She couldn't. Impossible to tell a man, any man, however nice he was, that you were trembling because your body for some totally unknown and embarrassing reason had suddenly decided that it found him so sexually desirable that your brain couldn't control its response to him.

Even now, her body was still reacting to him, her nipples taut and stiff, her stomach tight with a sensation she couldn't remember experiencing in years. How *could* she tell him any of that? How *could* she tell him that she had looked at his mouth and for one insane awful moment had not only wondered what it would feel like against her own, but had actually been in danger of leaning towards him; of physically betraying her yearning, aching need to experience his kiss?

She did not want him really, she assured herself. It was all because of Anna, because of Ian. Anna's cruel gibes about her lack of sexuality had gone deep and left a festering poison, which had somehow erupted in that appallingly embarrassing wave of heat and need, so that for a moment she had actively wanted to prove Anna wrong by...

By what...? Wanting Stuart to make love to her?

She was still trembling, shocked both by what she had experienced and her own ability to understand it.

'Sara.'

She heard the urgency, the concern in Stuart's voice.

'I ... I'm fine ...' she lied shakily.

She could tell from the way he was looking at her that he didn't believe her, but she was grateful to him when he didn't press her, simply lifting her down out of the Land Rover. And she needed his help now, she recognised weakly. She felt so disorientated, so feeble...so ...shocked and shaken by what she had just experienced.

As he swung her down to the ground, her hair brushed his face. She felt the sudden brief tension in his hands, before he set her down and released her.

'Nice perfume,' he commented, his voice almost rough, his face averted from her.

Perfume? She was puzzled.

'But I don't wear perfume. At least...' She had washed her hair this morning and she could only presume that it was her shampoo he could smell. It gave her an odd feeling in the pit of her stomach to know that he had been close enough to her to inhale the scent of her hair. What if she had inadvertently moved just that little bit closer to him...? Would she then have felt the warmth of his breath against her skin? Would he...?

'Look, if you want to change your mind... If you're not feeling up to this...'

She heard what he was saying and tried to focus on it, shaking her head in quick negation of his suggestion, telling him quickly, 'No, no. I'm fine.'

As he closed the Land Rover door she watched him, her glance sliding almost compulsively to his mouth. What if he had kissed her then when he was lifting her out of the Land Rover? What if he had actually read her mind and...?

She swallowed hard. She ought to be heartily glad that he had done no such thing. It was embarrassing enough as it was that she should actually have experienced those sensations, never mind having him recognise her vulnerability.

What was happening to her? she wondered in self-revulsion. All through the years when she had loved Ian, had wanted him, she had never been remotely interested in any other man, had never experienced the least desire for anyone else. And yet here she was...

It was just reaction, that was all—reaction to Anna's cruelty, reaction to reality... reaction to the discovery that she had wasted so many years in idiotic daydreams and fantasy. Her reaction to Stuart was undoubtedly only her body's way of desperately trying to prove that Anna had been wrong in telling her she was sexless and undesirable. Now that she was aware of her vulnerability she would be able to control and monitor it. There was no real reason for her to feel alarmed and apprehensive. Once she had thoroughly analysed and understood her uncharacteristic behaviour it wouldn't happen again.

Feeling a lot happier now that she had explained to her own satisfaction just why she had reacted in such an unexpected and potentially embarrassing fashion, she fell into step beside Stuart.

CHAPTER FOUR

'How about a quick tour of the house followed by lunch?' Stuart suggested once they were inside.

'Wouldn't you prefer me to look over your paperwork first?' Sara offered.

He smiled ruefully at her. 'I'm afraid to risk letting you see the chaos it's in on an empty stomach.'

'As bad as that?' Sara sympathised.

'Worse,' he assured her.

Sara laughed. She was getting to like him more and more. In fact she couldn't remember ever feeling so instantly at ease with anyone. If only she hadn't had that idiotic reaction to him while he was helping her out of the Land Rover. Thank goodness he at least hadn't realised the effect he was having on her.

'If you can just hang on for a sec while I get the lunch on, I'll do my best to act as an adequate tour guide. I expect you know more than I do about the house's history. One day when I've got rather more time to spare than I'm likely to have for quite some time to come I'd like to research the house's past more thoroughly, sort out the reality from the myths. It's changed hands so often.'

'Yes, I know,' Sara agreed, telling herself that it was ridiculous of her to feel an unmistakable if slight tinge of feminine chagrin at the efficient way he moved around the kitchen, deftly preparing the salmon for their lunch. She was all for men and women sharing their household tasks in theory, but in reality, much to her own astonishment, she was discovering that she felt a small *frisson* of resentment when confronted with the evidence that such a very male man was obviously completely self-sufficient.

Inwardly chiding herself, she asked herself sternly if she would really have preferred it if Stuart had sat back and expected her to take over the chore of making their lunch. Why should she want to? So that she could impress him with her domestic skills? How ridiculous. How...

'My cooking is pretty basic, I'm afraid,' Stuart told her, interrupting her thought-flow.

'It will just be salmon, new potatoes and green beans. Unfortunately my talents do not stretch as far as Hollandaise sauce.'

Sara's did. Her mother was a first-rate and very inspired cook, and she had passed on to both her daughters her pleasure in the preparation of food, even if Sara had discovered once she was living alone in London that, for her, most of the pleasure in cooking came from watching others eat what she had prepared for them.

Ian, even if they had been close enough for her to have asked him round for dinner, preferred to eat out, somewhere expensive and fashionable where the food he was eating was generally of little importance to him.

'Ready for the grand tour?' Stuart asked her, deftly placing the salmon in the oven and closing the door.

Nodding her head, Sara stood up.

'I thought we'd start at the top and work our way down,' Stuart suggested. 'We'll leave out the attics. They're filthy, for one thing.'

'How many bedrooms does the house have?' Sara asked him, as he stood back to allow her to precede him up what were obviously the back stairs.

'Twelve,' Stuart told her, 'but ultimately I'd like to reduce that to eight, and to use the smaller rooms as bathrooms. I'm not using it at the moment, because there was a problem with one of the windows, which over the years has led to quite considerable damp and deterioration in the plasterwork inside it, but the master bedroom has its own adjoining sitting-room, which I'd like to retain. I rather like the idea of having somewhere comfortable and private to relax in.'

'You could perhaps turn it into a sitting-room-cum-study,' Sara suggested, as they reached the landing. 'These days with computer terminals, and——'

'A computer terminal? No, thanks,' Stuart interrupted her firmly. 'Computers and I do not exactly see eye to eye.'

Sara laughed.

'Perhaps you're not using the right software. Now there are so many user-friendly——'

'It might be user-friendly, but I am most definitely not computer-friendly,' Stuart told her wryly. 'I know that isn't the sort of thing one ought to admit to these days, rather as in the past no male worthy of the name dared to admit that he couldn't drive a car. The animal I have now is supposed to be virtually able to do everything bar licking the stamps to put on the envelopes, but every time I attempt to use it...' He shrugged as he pushed open the first of the doors along the corridor.

It was a good-sized room, with three small windows, all of them barred.

'No doubt this must once have been used as a schoolroom or nursery,' he commented, as Sara walked over to the windows.

They overlooked the rear of the house, and beyond the wall encircling the stables and the yard she could see what must once have been the kitchen garden. This was totally enclosed by a high brick wall, with gates set into it. The area inside the wall was a tangle of weeds, nettles and overgrown briars.

'That's another of my future goals,' Stuart told her, coming to stand beside her. 'To restore the kitchen garden, if not to what it once was then at least to something a lot more productive than it is now. There must once have been a glasshouse along one of the walls, and espaliered fruit trees on the others.'

'Wouldn't it be very labour-intensive?' Sara asked him.

'Mmm. But if I expand as I hope to do there are bound to be quiet periods when men can be spared from working with the trees, to spend some time on the rest of the grounds. If not, I'll just have to make sure that if and when I marry my wife is a keen gardener.

'Do you like gardening?' he asked her.

It was a natural enough question, and of course had nothing to do with his preceding comment, especially when he had already indicated to her that he was still getting over a broken love-affair, and when he knew that she also... It was stupid of her

to feel so idiotically self-conscious, so vividly aware
of just how much she would have enjoyed spending
the lengthening spring days working within the
shelter of those ancient walls, digging,
planting...watching things grow...feeding and
nurturing her young crops, and then, later in the
year, enjoying the rewards of all her hard work as
she harvested their produce.

'Yes. Yes, I do,' she told him, conscious that both
her body and her voice were stiff with tension as
she turned away from the window and headed for
the door.

The rest of the house was very much as Stuart had
described it to her. He showed her where he had
made repairs to the exterior fabric of the building
in order to prevent leaks and rain damage, but, as
he told her, the house was going to require a good
deal of work doing on it before it could be described
as a home.

'Still, at least you know what *can* be done,' Sara
commented after Stuart had shown her the small
panelled study, pointing out where damp had
spoiled the woodwork. 'The work you've done on
the kitchen is marvellous.'

'Thank you. I'm not quite so confident of being
able to restore the original panelling and the stairs
quite so effectively. I suspect it's going to take a
good deal of searching through the reclamation
yards trying to find that elusive and all-important
exactly right item.'

'Hard work,' Sara agreed, 'but most definitely
worthwhile. In an odd sort of way I almost envy
you.'

He gave her a wry look.

'It's such a marvellous challenge, and even when you've got the house as you want it it isn't over; then you've got the pleasure of living here. Of knowing how much the effort you've put into it is making it what it is.'

'Not very many women would share that view,' Stuart told her drily, making her wonder if perhaps it could have been his decision to relocate here to the Welsh borders which had brought about the end of his love-affair.

Perhaps his Canadian girlfriend—she could only assume that she must have been Canadian, since he had already told her he had been working there— had not cared for the idea of moving to Britain and living in such an old and ramshackle building. Personally she could think of nothing she would enjoy more than the challenge the house represented. Even without closing her eyes she could already picture how it would one day look: rich brocades enhancing the mellow restored panelling, waxed floors, Persian rugs, sturdy pieces of oak furniture, some antique, some more modern, just as some of the rooms would be clothed in rare and valuable antiques while others would be furnished with more practical child-proof items. Off the kitchen, there would be a sunny, comfortable morning-room where children could play within earshot of their mother. Upstairs would be the master suite which Stuart had described, with its sturdy four-poster bed, its air of peace and tranquillity, its comfortable sitting-room, where husband and wife could retire to spend a few precious hours on their own: a private retreat whose existence was respected by all other members of the family, teenagers included.

Over lunch, Stuart described his work to her in a little more detail, causing her to marvel openly at what seemed to her to be his almost magical ability to uproot and transplant fully mature trees.

She laughed when he told her that he was just as impressed and bemused by her confidence in being able to restore order to his paperwork.

After they had had lunch, he reluctantly ushered her into his office, warning her that if, once she had seen the chaos that awaited her, she chose to change her mind and withdraw her offer of assistance, he would not blame her.

It was true that the office was untidy, but at least he had made some attempt to keep things in order, as he explained to her when he pointed out that the various apparently haphazard piles of paper on the desk each consisted of either incoming correspondence relating to orders, orders completed, those awaiting delivery, plus two other stacks of incoming and outgoing invoices.

When Sara pointed out to him that all of his problems could be reduced to much more manageable proportions if he made full use of his computer and set aside a small amount of time every day in order to keep on top of the paperwork as it arose, he asked her wryly, 'How small is a small amount of time? At the moment, I'm working flat out, outside.'

Sara eyed the desk thoughtfully, and pronounced, 'Well, at the moment I'd say you'd need to spend probably two or even three full days getting all this stuff on to the computer, and then—— '

'Don't go any further,' Stuart warned her. 'Two or three days, you say... I suspect you mean it would take *you* two or three days. It would take me more like two or three months.'

Sara laughed and asked him, 'Have you thought of employing someone on a part-time basis to cope with the paperwork for you?'

'Have I? Every time I walk in here—but you try getting someone qualified to deal with it, with all the skills that that involves, to come all the way out here, for the very small salary that's all I can afford to pay them.

'Look,' he added abruptly, 'I can't ask you to give up so much of your time. Not when you've come down here to——'

'To come to terms with the fact that Ian is never going to want me,' Sara supplied brittly. 'Believe me, something to keep my mind occupied is exactly what I *do* need.' She broke off, wondering if she had said too much, if his comment had perhaps been a tactful way of telling her that he had changed his mind on realising how long it would take her to get things in order, and was tactfully refusing her offer of assistance as he did not want to have her spending so much time in his home.

But to her surprise he said almost tersely, 'Well, if that really is the case, how about working for me on a part-time basis while you're here? I know you said you'd probably be staying for a few months. As I've already said, I can't afford to pay you a great deal, certainly nothing like the amount you're worth, but if you do genuinely want something to fill in some of your time...'

Work for Stuart. She gnawed thoughtfully on her bottom lip and then released it with a small wince of pain, telling herself that nibbling on it every time she was anxious about something was a habit she really must break.

'I'm sorry,' Stuart was apologising. 'I really shouldn't have suggested it. Of course you don't——'

'No. No. I do.' Sara corrected him quickly. 'I was just worried that you might have offered me the job because...because you...you felt sorry for me.'

She flushed as she made the admission.

It didn't matter how well she got on with him, he was still a man, and as a man couldn't be expected to understand the legacy of insecurity and doubt about her own femininity, her sexuality, her deepest emotions and feelings about being a woman. He couldn't be expected to know how much Anna's gibes had damaged and maimed her, had left her unable to have any faith in herself as a woman...had left her feeling that there was something lacking in her, some vital part or ingredient. It had destroyed her confidence in herself, her faith in her ability to function as a woman in the fullest sensual sense.

'You think I'm offering you a job out of pity?' Stuart shook his head and told her almost grimly, 'Out of *self*-pity, maybe, but not out of pity for you. I *don't* pity you. As a matter of fact, I still think you've had a lucky escape. The man must be a fool to let a woman like you——'

He broke off and then continued roughly, 'Take it from me, if you decide to work for me, *you'll* be the one doing me the favour, not the other way round.'

Caution urged her to say that she needed time to think about it, to consider, but instinct urged her to go ahead and accept his offer. A means of occupying her mind was exactly what she needed right now. If she hesitated, started allowing herself to have doubts...

'I would like to work for you,' she told him firmly before she could change her mind. 'If you're sure that that's what you want.'

'What I want?' He gave her an odd, almost brooding look, before telling her incomprehensibly, 'Well, it's a start. If you're ready I'll show you round outside now. You brought your Wellingtons? I know it's a fine day, but...'

'I was brought up here, remember,' Sara reminded him. 'They're still in your Land Rover.'

'Right, you hang on here. I'll go and get them for you, and then we'll make a start.'

He was opening the kitchen door before she could protest that she was perfectly capable of getting them for herself. As she watched him striding across the yard to the Land Rover, she asked herself if she had done the right thing in accepting his offer of a job. Still, it was too late to rescind her decision now, and besides...besides... She discovered with a mild thrill of shock that she was actually almost looking forward to working here, to the challenge.

'Of what? Sorting out his paperwork?' A small uneasy sensation stirred in the pit of her stomach. She wasn't one of those idiotic women who got themselves involved in an endlessly repetitive, destructive cycle, was she? She wasn't going to allow herself to develop the same kind of emotional dependence on Stuart that she had developed on Ian . . .?

No, of course she wasn't. The two men were completely different; the two situations were completely different. She had been in love with Ian before she went to work with him. She wasn't remotely in danger of falling in love with Stuart. How could she be when she still loved Ian?

Ian. It was only when she had her Wellingtons on and was walking beside Stuart towards the Land Rover that she realised how little she had thought about Ian in the past few hours.

A tiny shiver struck her, but she subdued it. That was good, wasn't it? That was the whole purpose in her coming home, here to the place where Ian had never been; where there were no memories of him to torment and taunt her.

Almost an hour later she stood silent with awe, in front of one of a dozen mature oak trees which, Stuart was just explaining to her, were due to be lifted and transplanted to an estate in the south of England which had lost many of its own mature trees in the gales which now seemed so much more common.

'In some cases, if we act fast enough, it is possible to save those trees which the gale has uprooted. Adolescent trees are the most at risk; they've got the height without the width of a secure root-base to support them, but, being adolescent, they very often have the resilience and ability to reroot themselves once we've replanted them, provided we act in time.'

The more he explained to her about his business, the more fascinating Sara found it. She had never realised it was such a complex subject, imagining that once a tree had been blown down and uprooted it had no real chance of survival.

'Mind out,' Stuart warned her, taking hold of her arm and helping her out of the way, as a miniature tractor-cum-trailer swung into view driven by a young man whom she recognised as the son of a local farmer.

When he smiled at her, she responded, causing Stuart to comment, 'You obviously know young Lewis Llewellyn.'

'Yes,' Sara agreed, watching as the young man swung the tractor expertly round the bend in the cart track, carefully manoeuvring the trailer with its load of young saplings.

'He's been working for me for a month or so now and he's doing very well. There isn't time today for me to show you the nursery where we're growing the young saplings, but now that you're coming to work here...'

He turned round as he spoke, but as Sara turned to follow him she forgot about the low overhanging branch close to her, and gasped in pain and shock as she pushed against its pliancy and it sprang back, whipping across her face.

Stuart heard her cry out and turned round, exclaiming, 'What is it? What's wrong?' Comprehension darkened his eyes as he saw the red weal marking her skin and read the message of pain given off by her body.

'Hell, that's my fault. I should have warned you. Here, let me have a look.'

Before she could stop him, he was cupping her face in his hands, turning it gently into the light, his body so close to her own that she could smell not only the fresh outdoors scent of the wind and growing things, but also the unmistakable warm male scent of his body.

Previously if anyone had even suggested to her that she could actually find in such an intimate awareness of a man's personal body scent something so erotic that her own flesh responded to it immediately and overwhelmingly she would have denied it vehemently, almost shocked by such a suggestion, and yet now, despite the stinging pain in her face, she discovered that she had actually taken a step towards Stuart, that she was actually eager to breathe in the intimate scent of him, that she was even wondering what it would be like to unfasten the buttons of his shirt, to slide her hands over the damp heat of his body, to rest her face against his skin, to...

She made a small protesting sound of denial of what she was experiencing, causing Stuart to apologise and tell her, 'I'm sorry. I know it must sting, but fortunately it doesn't seem to have lacerated the skin. It *is* grazed, though, and I think we'd better get you back to the house and get some antiseptic on it. I should have warned you about that branch.'

'It's my own fault,' Sara told him shakily. He was still standing closer to her, his hands still cupping her face. She wanted him to release her. She was all too uncomfortably conscious of her awareness of him. It made her feel guilty; she had no right to feel so intimately aware of him...no right and no reason. What was the matter with her? Had Ian's rejection of her changed her so completely that she had gone almost overnight from being a woman with very little interest in or awareness of male sexuality to a woman who was so acutely aware of it, so embarrassingly responsive to it that instead of moving away from Stuart as she ought to be doing she was having to fight against an overwhelming urge to move closer to him?

He had been wearing a pair of heavy-duty working gloves. Now he pulled one of them off and ran his thumb gently over the abrasion, causing her to wince and shiver.

'I'm sorry,' he apologised again. 'I just wanted to check that you are only grazed and that no bark has lodged in the wound.'

As he spoke, the breeze caught hold of her hair and whipped it across his face. He moved his hand, sliding it against her scalp, lifting it back behind her ear.

As his hand touched her skin, she shivered violently. She felt the tension that suddenly held him still and lifted her gaze to his.

His eyes were darkly gold, glittering fiercely, tension drawing the flesh of his face taut against his bones. His eyelids dropped, hiding his expression from her, his lashes thick and dark against his tanned skin.

He was looking, she realised with stomach-lurching intensity, at her mouth.

Immediately she was conscious of a desire to wet her lips with her tongue-tip; she was equally aware of the swollen fullness of her bottom lip where she had bitten it.

'You've bitten your lip.'

The words seemed to reach her from a great distance, slow and heavy, as though each one was weighed down with great importance.

'Yes. It's a bad habit.'

Now she did touch her bottom lip with her tongue-tip, finding the small wound she herself had inflicted.

'Don't.'

The raw command made her stiffen as she automatically searched his face, her eyes dazed and confused.

He was lowering his head, moving closer to her. There was still time for her to move away, still time for her to avoid the kiss she knew was coming, but although she trembled and felt the mingling of excitement and apprehension burning through her veins like a powerful drug she made no attempt to move away.

He kissed her gently, tenderly almost, his mouth warm and explorative on hers, his tongue-tip finding the small abrasion on her bottom lip and stroking it, soothing it, and then suddenly and overwhelmingly filling her with such a sharp piercing response to him that she was opening her mouth, reaching out towards him, moving eagerly within the circle of his arms almost before she knew what she was doing.

She could feel the fierce almost frantic thud of his heart against her body, smell the warm aroused man scent of him, feel the tautness of his body, its alien maleness, its strength and power, and such a force of need—of yearning...of aching...

wanting—filled her that her awareness of it shocked her into realising what she was doing... what she was feeling. She made a small moan of protest beneath his mouth, pushing against his chest, so that he immediately released her and stepped back from her.

'I'm sorry.'

A hard flush of colour ran along his cheekbones; he looked almost grimly angry—not with her, Sara realised guiltily, as he made a stilted apology, but with himself.

'I haven't any excuse. There *is* no excuse. I should never have...' His mouth twisted. 'All I can hope is that you'll be generous and put it down to the fact that you are a very attractive and desirable woman, and I'm a man who has perhaps been living on his own for too long.'

What *could* she say? If he was guilty then so was she. She had *known* he was going to kiss her, had known it and had done nothing whatsoever to prevent it, which she could have done. Just a simple step back from him... just a simple turning away of her head, and the whole situation could have been easily averted, but instead... She took a deep breath, acknowledging inwardly that not only had she wanted him to kiss her, but she had almost actively invited and encouraged it. Even if he had not recognised her responsiveness to him, and it seemed that he had not, she most certainly had.

As she turned her head away from him, she heard him saying quietly, 'I hope this won't affect your decision to come and work for me. I promise you that it won't happen again. Now that I'm aware...'

She froze, tensing her muscles, afraid that he might after all have recognised that it could have been her own awareness of him which had somehow been indirectly responsible for his reaction to her; that he might after all have recognised it but been too good-mannered to mention it, but to her relief he broke off, looking grimly into the middle distance, leaving her to say into the heavy silence, 'Please don't apologise. After all, we're both mature adults. I'm sure both of us realise that it...that is...' She was beginning to flounder a little, guiltily aware of how fast her heart was beating, of how she could still feel the warmth of his mouth on her own, of how intensely a part of her longed still to actually have his mouth on her own.

'...that it was just a reflex physical reaction,' she stammered lamely.

He gave her a sharply direct look that made her skin flush with discomfort and guilt. 'A reflex physical reaction. Yes, I suppose you're right.'

For some reason his comment hurt her. What would she have preferred him to say? she derided herself half an hour later as he drove the Land Rover back into the cobbled yard. That he had been overwhelmed by desire for her? That he had felt a momentary and uncontrollable male lust for her? Of course not. She was allowing Ian's rejection of her to make her wallow in self-pity, to make her want some kind of ridiculous show of male desire for her—any male desire. She ought to be disgusted with herself, ashamed of herself, instead of feeling...

She bit down hard on her bottom lip, wincing as she caught the broken flesh.

Instead of feeling what? Cheated...deprived...all too conscious of that small sharp ache inside her body which said that if she hadn't been stupid enough to push him away Stuart might well have...

Have what? Made love to her? Of course he wouldn't and of course she wouldn't have wanted him to. The very idea was...

She swallowed hard, unwilling to admit exactly what her reaction to the very idea of Stuart making love to her was.

'I'd better take a proper look at that graze,' Stuart told her as he stopped the Land Rover.

'There's no need,' Sara assured him hastily. 'It feels fine now... Would it be OK if I stayed on for a couple of hours? I'd like to familiarise myself with your computer, and go through the paperwork with you, but if I'm going to be in the way I could leave it until...'

'You won't be in the way,' Stuart told her, but his voice was terse, and his earlier warmth and friendliness seemed to have chilled—or was she being absurdly sensitive, looking for problems, for rebuffs that in all probability did not exist? *Had* she allowed Ian's rejection to make her so sensitive...too sensitive? After all, Stuart was the one who had asked for her help, who had suggested that she come and work for him.

The fact that he had kissed her... Sara swallowed, unhappily aware of the fact that this time, although he came round to her side of the Land Rover and opened the door for her, he made no attempt to physically help her down, even though he waited politely until she was safely on the ground.

The fact that he had kissed her was something she would be well advised to put completely out of her mind. What had it been other than an automatic male reaction to the proximity of a female?

Nothing. And it was obvious that Stuart had regretted the impulse almost as quickly as it had formed. Well, of course he would regret it, wouldn't he? She had already gathered that he, like her, had lost someone he loved. Obviously as a man he still felt all the normal male sexual desires and needs . . . and just as obviously he had no wish for her to misinterpret his momentary reaction to her.

After what she had told him about Ian, he was probably concerned that she might be the kind of woman who made a habit of falling in love with her boss. Well, if so it was up to her to convince him otherwise . . . or to tell him that she had changed her mind about working for him.

But she wanted this job, needed it . . . not for the money, but for the mental stimulation, for its ability to keep her mind off Ian and the past.

The most sensible thing she could do was to show Stuart that what had happened this afternoon meant nothing whatsoever to her, that she fully understood that it had been a momentary aberration and that as such it was something best forgotten by both of them.

CHAPTER FIVE

'TIME to take a break. I've made some coffee and there's toast in the kitchen if you want it.'

Sara looked up from the VDU, frowning slightly as she focused on Stuart.

She had been so deeply engrossed in what she was doing that she hadn't even heard the door open, but now that he had mentioned coffee she realised how much she was longing for a cup, and as for the toast... Her stomach made a gently discreet protest, reminding her that it had been several hours since lunchtime.

'That sounds great,' she told him, turning away from the screen and stretching her torso, relaxing her taut muscles.

'I hardly dare ask how it's going,' Stuart told her five minutes later when they were both seated at the kitchen table.

'It's going well,' Sara assured him. 'The software is good, the program fairly flexible, although I must confess it is a little advanced perhaps for a beginner.'

'There's no need to be tactful,' Stuart told her ruefully. 'When it comes to growing trees, I pride myself on knowing what I'm doing, and I'm likely to take umbrage if anyone says otherwise. When it comes to handling a computer, we're in a different ballgame altogether.'

Over their coffee and toast, Sara explained to him as simply as she could what she intended to do, whilst he listened and watched her ruefully, commenting when she had finished, 'If I were that boss of yours, I'd be beating a path to your parents' door, and begging you to come back...' He broke off, shaking his head. 'I'm sorry,' he told her. 'I wasn't thinking. I didn't mean...'

'It's all right,' Sara told him shakily. 'I've already accepted that Ian and all I'd hoped to share with him is in the past. It was all an idiotic dream anyway. I'm beginning to realise now that even if he *had* loved me it would never have worked.'

She saw Stuart was frowning, and explained wryly, 'We're too different—our views on life, our values. I'm still very much a country woman at heart. I would want to bring my children up somewhere like this, somewhere, *anywhere* other than in a city, especially a city like London; whereas Ian, even if he had agreed to have children, would have expected me to hand them over to a nanny. He loves city life. He loves being at the centre of everything. He would loathe living somewhere like this, and he's the kind of man——' She broke off, biting her lip, not wanting to admit what she was coming to realise: that Ian was too shallow, too vain ever to be the kind of man who could bear to be anything other than the centre of a woman's life. Children to him would be competitors, rivals. He would expect and demand always to come first, and, while she believed that a woman's relationship with her husband, the father of her children, must always be special and treasured, there were bound to be times when the claims of a family, especially a young family, might mean that adult relationships and needs must take second place.

'It sounds to me as though you're better off without him,' Stuart told her grimly.

'Yes,' Sara agreed. 'I expect I am. Not that I ever actually had him.' She stopped, flushing a brilliant shade of crimson, as she realised the sexual connotations unwittingly carried by her remark, but Stuart seemed to be unaware of her embarrassment and the reason for it as he turned away from her, asking calmly,

'Fancy another cup of coffee?'

By the time she had accepted, and he had poured it, her colour had gone back to normal and to her relief he seemed to have lost interest in the subject of Ian, and returned instead to the problems he had been having in mastering his computer.

'Sally thought it was hilarious when I told her I was buying it,' he confided.

Sally? Sara felt her heart lurch. Who was Sally? Or could she guess? Was she the mystery woman who had deserted him, who had allowed him to love her and who had then rejected him? Already she disliked her. Her laughter held painful echoes of Anna's laughter, Anna's cruelty.

'Did she? Wasn't that a little insensitive of her?' Sara demanded. Something about the rueful warmth in Stuart's voice as he mentioned the other woman increased her antipathy towards her, although she couldn't really understand why, other than that she felt quite extraordinarily protective towards him. As a fellow victim? She doubted that Stuart would ever have behaved as stupidly as she had done. Despite his kindness, his warmth, his niceness, there was a very evident toughness about him; a maleness that suggested that he could when necessary be an extremely formidable foe. Only he and this Sally hadn't been foes, had they? They had been lovers.

Lovers... She swallowed painfully. Her eyes had started to ache and burn. Too long spent staring at the VDU, she told herself, totally ignoring the fact that in the course of a normal day's work she spent far longer than she had done today engaged in that very same task—but it couldn't be tears... *emotional* pain that was making her eyes sting, could it?

She couldn't really possibly be jealous of this Sally. No, of course she couldn't. Perhaps a little envious... Not of her relationship with Stuart, but of the fact that she had known what it was like to have a lover, to experience a man's desire, his physical compulsion to show her how much he loved and wanted her.

She had never known that... and now probably never would. At twenty-nine she was quite definitely far too old to experience the intensity of such passion, such love, and even if she did... She shivered a little. No, she didn't want ever again to feel for someone else what she had felt for Ian. It was too dangerous, too destructive. Margaret had been right: what she ought to do was to form a nice safe relationship with a quiet pleasant man who, like herself, wanted to settle down, to marry and have children. A man with whom she could live in quiet comfort without the highs and lows of passion and love.

'Stop thinking about him. There's no point in tearing yourself apart——'

'Over a man who doesn't want me,' Sara supplied drearily. 'No, you're right. Although, as a matter of fact, I wasn't thinking about Ian.' She drank her coffee and stood up.

'I'd better get on. I've still got quite a bit to do before I call it a day...'

As she walked towards the door, she was suddenly acutely conscious of the fact that Stuart was watching her, although why she should be so aware of his silent regard now, after the time they had spent together, she really had no idea.

Sara worked on the computer for another hour, before feeling that she had come to a point where she could reasonably stop.

Stuart had invited her to join him for supper, but she had refused his invitation to allow him to take her out for dinner as a thank-you for the work she had done, pointing out that if she was going to work for him he could not be expected to provide her with meals as well as a salary.

A little later, when he drove her back to her parents' home, he seemed rather withdrawn. Had she offended him by refusing his offer of dinner? Surely not. As she contemplated the solitude of the evening that lay ahead of her, she half wished that she had after all accepted.

She would have enjoyed his company. There would not have been any stilted pauses in their conversation. He might be a man who preferred to work out of doors, but from the books she had seen in his study and sitting-room, from the conversations she had already had with him, she knew already that he was a man with very widespread interests.

The kind of man, in fact, whom any sane woman would have been only too delighted to have as a dinner companion, or as a lover.

She stiffened, resisting the thought as she had resisted it the previous evening. What on earth was the matter with her? In the days when her thoughts, when her life, had revolved entirely around Ian, it had never crossed her mind to think of any other man in terms of his sexuality, but now...

The moment Stuart brought the Land Rover to a halt, she opened the door and started to scramble out, without waiting for him to come round to her side of the vehicle and assist her.

The illumination from the security lights which had sprung on when they stopped showed her that his mouth had compressed in a grimly bitter line, giving him an air of distance and withdrawal, making her want to reach out to him, and beg him not to look at her so coldly.

She found that she was actually shivering as though the temperature had dropped by several degrees.

It dismayed her that she should be so distressed by Stuart's apparent change of mood, and as he walked her to the door she was conscious of a very strong need to close the gap between them and to move closer to his body, something which astonished her since she was normally by nature the kind of person who preferred to keep a definite physical distance between herself and others.

At her door she paused and turned to face him, saying quickly, 'If it's all right with you, I'll start work at ten tomorrow and stay on until about three.'

'You still want the job, then?'

'Yes,' she assured him vehemently, 'Unless... unless you've changed your mind.'

'No.' He sounded abrupt, irritated almost. 'I'll probably be out when you arrive. I'll leave the back door unlocked for you. We'll have to sort out something about a key.'

He paused and Sara looked up at him. She was standing far closer to him than she had realised, and a tiny but unmistakable quiver of sensation darted through her body. She looked quickly away to avoid the temptation of focusing on his mouth. Thank goodness he had no idea of the effect he was having on her. She could barely comprehend it herself, and could only put it down to some kind of extraordinary and totally out-of-character reaction to the wounds inflicted by Ian and Anna; a desperate and reactionary attempt by her body to prove them wrong when they'd described her as sexless. Whatever was causing it, she hoped that it would soon stop.

It was only later as she was eating her supper that she realised that the only occasion during the day on which she had thought about Ian had been in conjunction with her awareness and responsiveness to Stuart, which must surely mean that she had made the right decision in returning home; that it *was* going to be easier to put the past behind her here than it would have been in London.

Stuart's offer of a job was an additional bonus which she had not expected. Not only would it help to pass the time, it would also give her an outlet for her mental energy; give her something on which to focus other than Ian and the pain he had caused her.

And as for her extraordinary and embarrassing reaction to Stuart as a man... Well, that would begin to fade, she was sure, once her emotions began to recover from the blows they had been dealt.

CHAPTER SIX

ONE week passed and then another. Her parents had returned, and her mother had been delighted to learn that she intended to stay at home for an indefinite period and even more delighted with the information that she was working for Stuart.

Her mother, as Sara quickly discovered, liked Stuart very much indeed. She had never met Ian, but Sara knew from her reaction to the news that she had given up her job with him that her parents were not sorry that he was no longer a part of her life.

Nothing had been said about her real reason for handing in her notice. If her parents had guessed how she had felt about him they were being very tactful in not saying so.

For the first few days after their return home, the new baby and their existing two grandsons had been the main topic of their conversation.

They had taken photographs so that Sara could see her new niece who, her mother assured her, was the very image of how she herself had been at exactly the same age.

Privately Sara suspected that her mother was exaggerating, but wisely she said nothing, carefully returning the photographs to their wallet, and trying to suppress the tiny ache in her heart. She loved her sister and liked her brother-in-law, but this was the first time she had actively found herself envying her sister. Two healthy boisterous sons and now a little girl, and Jacqui was after all only five years her senior.

She reminded herself that she was still not thirty, and that there was plenty of time for her to settle down and marry, but the ache inside her body when she looked at the photographs of her new niece warned her that her instincts were growing impatient with her...that her need and desire for children were daily growing more urgent, more powerful. So much so that more and more often she found she was turning over in her mind Margaret's advice to her. She had loved Ian all her adult life, but Ian didn't want her, would never want her, and she could not in all honesty visualise herself allowing herself to fall in love again. It had proved too painful, been too self-destructive. No, she didn't want to take the risk of falling in love again, but neither did she want to give up her dreams of having children. Which meant...which meant that perhaps she ought to take Margaret's advice: to start thinking seriously about a relationship founded on something that would be far less exciting, far less idealistic than falling in love with Ian.

She frowned, remembering how at Christmas, before the blow had fallen, when she had returned from her parents' to London and had been invited round to Margaret's to view the children's Christmas presents, Ben had remarked what a good mother she would make, and she had admitted how much she loved and wanted a family. Obliquely, or so it had seemed then, Margaret had commented that she could not see Ian taking well to fatherhood.

Then her denial of Margaret's comment had been instinctive and automatic, but now she was forced to realise that it had been the truth, and that a part of her had always known this, and yet despite that, despite the fact that in so many ways their outlooks on life were totally in conflict, she had stubbornly gone on clinging to her idiotic daydreams, to her hopes.

She had been a fool, she recognised, and worse... she had stubbornly and self-destructively ignored what her common sense had often tried to tell her: that Ian, no matter how much she was in love with him, was not really someone with whom she could ever truly live in harmony.

Well, one thing was certain, she told herself humorously. She wasn't going to have much chance of finding herself a potential husband and father for her children while she was working for Stuart.

She had now reduced the chaos of his paperwork to something approaching order. She was waiting for him to produce for her written lists of his stock, which she intended to categorise into type, age, height, et cetera, so that in future when he received enquiries for trees a mere flick on the computer would be able to furnish him with a printed list of this information on demand.

When she had pointed this out to him, he had grinned at her, and pointed out that he already carried all this information in his head.

It had been hard not to share his amusement. She had told him severely that he wasn't super-human and that there might well come a day when for one reason or another he was not available when such information was required.

She was getting on better and better with him as she came to know him better. They shared a similar sense of humour; a deep love of the countryside, and the need to preserve and maintain it. Stuart had already been approached to sit on several local conservation committees, and, as he had told her, now that she had tamed his paperwork he hoped to have the time to play a much larger part in the affairs of their small community.

Somehow or other, the four hours a day which they had agreed Sara would work had extended to six and then sometimes closer to eight, as she willingly took on more and more of the indoor running of the business. It pleased her that Stuart was so prepared to trust her, and she found she enjoyed the challenge of expanding her knowledge and making use of it.

By the time she had worked with him for a month, she was able to talk with awareness and authority to would-be customers about the feasibility of transplanting a variety of trees, calmly soothing their fears that such mature wood could not be safely moved.

A date had been fixed for the christening of her new niece, and, a little to her consternation, her mother had insisted on issuing Stuart with an invitation to share in the celebration with them.

Ignoring her own protest to her mother that she was sure that Stuart had far better things to do, he calmly accepted. When he was free to do so, he had taken to picking her up in the morning and running her home at night, claiming that it was unfair to expect her to risk damage to her own car on the rough lane that led to the manor.

She could of course have insisted on remaining independent, but the truth was that she enjoyed his company too much to do so, just as she enjoyed those evenings when work kept her at the manor until quite late, and Stuart insisted on making supper for them both.

The evenings were growing lighter now, which meant that Stuart was out working on the estate for longer and longer periods of time, so that often during the day she found she was seeing less of him, although there were frequently occasions when he would arrive unexpectedly at the house and invade the office, demanding her company outside, so that he could show her some new aspect of his work which she hadn't yet seen.

She had grown so used to these excursions that she now kept a spare pair of Wellingtons and her old Barbour up at the manor, ready to put on when she accompanied him outside.

Every morning Stuart received a delivery of national papers which included *The Times*, and Sara normally glanced through these while she was having her lunch.

Initially it had been her intention to go home at lunchtime, since she was conscious of the fact that in addition to being his place of work the manor was also Stuart's home, and that, no matter how politely he might deny it, he could well prefer not to find her curled up in a chair in front of the range eating her lunch on those occasions when he came back to the house for his. However, within a couple of weeks of her starting to work for him he had told her one day that if it was the thought of his presence in the house intruding into her lunch-hour and her free time which was preventing her from staying then he was quite prepared not to return to the house during the day. By the time she had assured him that this was most definitely not the case she had also discovered that she had agreed that yes, it would be far more sensible for her to stay on at the manor during her lunch-hour, so that she was on hand to answer the phone should it ring.

On this particular day she had found a very relevant and absorbing article in *The Times* on the global greenhouse effect, and the devastation wreaked by the previous spring's storms on wooded areas of the country. Mention was made in the article of the fact that it was now possible to replace storm-damaged trees with mature broadleaved specimens, and it was just as Sara was searching for a pen to mark the article for Stuart's attention that she happened to glance at the opposite page.

Why, out of all the notices on that page, her glance should immediately fall on the announcement of Anna's and Ian's engagement and forthcoming marriage, she really had no idea, but once she *had* seen it she remained transfixed in her chair, unable to drag her gaze away from the heavy black print.

She heard the back door opening as Stuart came in, but lacked the will-power to look up from the paper. She could feel her whole body trembling, but knew that she wasn't cold.

She heard Stuart speak to her, and was distantly aware of the sharpening concern in his voice as he repeated her name and then came striding across to where she was sitting, demanding, 'Sara, what is it? What's wrong?'

The sound of his voice, the concern that roughened it, her awareness of his proximity, of the warmth and comfort of his physical presence, broke through her icy guard. She could feel the numbness which had frozen her when she'd read the announcement giving way to a deep welling of emotional release; to tears which clogged her throat and filled her eyes, so that when she tried to focus on him he gave a sharp exclamation, and then reached for her, homing in on what she had read before firmly removing the newspaper from her grasp and flinging it down on to the table before taking her in his arms as though it were something he had done on so many previous occasions that it was an automatic unthinking response to her pain.

As though it were the most natural thing in the world, Sara clung to him, allowing him to draw her to her feet and wrap her in his arms, gently rocking her against him as he soothed her with rough words of compassion and comfort.

'The man's a fool,' she heard him saying grittily. 'He must be, to prefer someone else, *anyone* else to you . . .'

That made her laugh, albeit rather shakily, as she struggled to deny his championship.

'What is it? What's wrong?' he demanded, as he felt her shaking her head.

'It isn't Ian's fault that he loves Anna and not me,' she told him. 'The blame's mine, for allowing myself to believe . . .' She bit her lip, unable to admit even to him how much the cruel truths Anna had told had hurt her and still continued to hurt her.

'It isn't just the fact that he's marrying someone else, is it?' he asked her perceptively.

Sara stared at him, her eyes wide and questioning. How had he known?

He was still holding her, her body pressed into the warmth of his as she arched her back so that she could look at him.

'How did you know——?' She broke off, flushing a little. 'I...It's the things Anna said to me. Realities...truths.' She gave a small shudder and felt his arms tighten as though he wanted to absorb the pain from her.

'What realities? What truths?'

She turned her head away from him and into his shoulder. Caution and shyness made her hesitate a fraction before responding to him, but the shock of seeing the announcement had weakened her defences, strengthened her fears, her self-doubts.

'When Anna...when she told me that Ian...that she and Ian knew how I felt about him, she laughed at me; told me that even if Ian had not fallen in love with her he would never have wanted me. That no man would ever want me...because... because...because I was sexless...undesirable...' She broke off, her voice thickening with emotion, her head virtually resting on Stuart's shoulder. She couldn't bear to look at him, dreading the pity she suspected she would see in his eyes. He had become more than an employer to her now. He had become a friend, a very good friend... her first really close male friend, but, while she sensed that he would view her revelations with sympathy and compassion, she now felt embarrassed and confused by the fact that she had made them. What was happening to her? Had she really changed so much in such a short space of time? The woman she had always thought herself to be would never have dreamed of confiding such information to anyone, much less a man, and yet curiously, despite her embarrassment, there was a sense of relief, of release in having done so...a sense of having jettisoned a burden which had grown progressively heavier.

'And you believed her?'

The rough disbelief in his voice jolted her into turning her head to look enquiringly at him.

'Can't you see? She *wanted* to hurt you. She was *lying* to you.'

'No. I——'

'She was *lying* to you,' Stuart insisted. 'And I can prove it to you. You're not sexless, Sara. Nor undesirable. In fact...'

She felt the tremor that tensed his body, confusion shocking through her as he muttered something under his breath and then lifted one of his hands from her body to her face, sliding it along her jaw, angling her face towards his own.

'Does this feel as if you're undesirable?' he demanded thickly against her mouth, and then he was kissing her with a sensual roughness that swept away her resistance.

Once, a long time ago, she had dreamed of being kissed like this, her lover a faceless, formless figment of her teenage imagination, his touch, his kiss unknown and unexperienced, and yet she had known that it could be like this; that one day it *would* be like this...that one day he would come into her life, and that when he did his touch, his

kiss would set a light to her sexuality, burning away
her virginal fears and apprehensions; and then she
had met Ian, and had put away such childish daydreams, focusing instead on the reality of the person
with whom she had fallen in love.

In those early years when she had first met him,
she had ached for Ian to kiss her, yearned for his
touch, imagining that when he did so it would be
as it had been in her daydreams, and yet when
eventually he had done so the reality had fallen so
far short of what she had imagined she would feel
that she had immediately decided that the fault lay
with her in foolishly believing that it could be
possible for a mere kiss to thrill her so much that
it would be a complete ravishment of all of her
being; that it would open for her a magic doorway
through which she would step into a place that was
a feast of all the senses.

Instead she had found Ian's kiss practised and
polished, but somehow unexciting.

She remembered this now while her senses spun
and her heart leapt in shocked recognition of all
that she was experiencing. She remembered as well
how she had loyally denied reality and deceived
herself into believing that Ian's kiss had been all
that she had wanted it to be.

She remembered also how she had waited for him
to follow it up with an avowal of his growing
feelings for her, and how cheated she had felt when,
although he continued to tease and kiss her on odd
occasions, he had never tried to take their relationship any further.

His treatment of her had left her feeling cheated
and insecure...unsure of herself and her

femininity...guilty because she wanted so much more from him than he seemed to want to give...blaming herself with hindsight for not giving him more encouragement, clinging stupidly to her hope that one day things would change, that one day he would love her.

For so long she had existed on mere crumbs that she might have felt that the feast of pleasure she was now experiencing was too rich a diet for her system, but her senses were overriding her mental warning of caution, hungrily feeding on the pleasure Stuart was giving them.

He hadn't done anything other than kiss her, but her body was responding to him as intensely as though he had touched it so intimately that none of its secrets was unknown to him.

That knowledge shocked her into tensing within his hold, causing him to lift his mouth from hers, and demand hoarsely, 'Try telling me *now* that you don't believe you're desirable.'

She moved restlessly against him, confused and shocked by what had happened. 'There was no need,' she began helplessly, hating the thought that he pitied her so much that he had somehow or other forced himself to simulate a desire for her which she knew he could not possibly feel...

'On the contrary, there was every need,' he told her flatly, confirming her fear.

She wriggled free of him, and turned her back to him.

'It was kind of you, but...' Her stifled voice broke.

'Kind of me!' She winced as Stuart swore. 'Are you really so obsessed by him that you can't see, don't know...? What is it you're hoping for, Sara? That he's going to change his mind? That he's going to come looking for you, begging you——?'

'No... No, of course I'm not,' she denied truthfully, flinching back from the pain his curt words were causing her. 'I'm not a fool. I know that isn't going to happen. I know I've got to get on with my life. I'd even begun to decide that Margaret was right when she told me I ought to look round for some like-minded man to settle down with. Someone who, like me, wants a family and is prepared to accept——'

'Second-best?' Stuart supplied brutally for her, making her wince again.

'Not necessarily,' she told him unevenly, 'providing we were honest with one another right from the start...providing we both knew and understood that——'

'That you loved someone else. Do you really want children so much?'

She paused, and then looked at him and said simply and bravely, 'Yes. Yes, I do...'

There was a small pause, and then he said heavily, 'I've got to get back to the men, but first——' He reached over to the table and picked up the paper, ripping the page carrying the announcement in two and then in half again, and then opening the door of the range and throwing the screwed-up sections into its heat.

'Why don't you take the rest of the day off?' he suggested gruffly, when the resultant flames had died.

Sara shook her head. 'No. I won't, if you don't mind. I'll be better off keeping myself occupied.'

* * *

Oddly, once he had gone and she was back in the office, supposedly compiling information regarding the various stages of growth in the newly planted nursery beds, it wasn't Ian who kept interrupting her work, and causing her to stare unseeingly into space, but Stuart himself.

Once she touched her mouth with curious, trembling fingers, her body going hot and softly fluid as her senses conjured up for her the sensations she had experienced when he'd kissed her.

She was still trembling minutes later even though she had snatched her hand away from her mouth as guiltily as a small child caught with its fingers in the biscuit barrel.

She couldn't understand what was happening to her, couldn't reach out and take a firm grasp of the at times nebulous, and at other times astonishingly powerful and strong feelings she was experiencing so that she could hold on to them and subject them to the calming influence of logical analysis.

She couldn't understand why it was that when Stuart kissed her—Stuart whom she had come to regard as a friend and companion—she should feel this powerful upsurge of desire and sexual responsiveness, of almost swooning need to experience even more intimacy with him, while when Ian had kissed her—Ian whom she loved—she was left with a sharp sense of disappointment, of an awareness of dissatisfaction and emptiness.

At half-past five, when Stuart hadn't returned, she was guiltily conscious of the fact that her work output had fallen far below her own high standards, and that she had spent by far the major proportion of her mental energy in trying to solve the mystery of why Stuart's touch, Stuart's kiss should affect her in the way it did.

At six o'clock she tidied up her desk and got ready to go home, cowardly aware that half of her was anxious and confused at the thought of seeing Stuart while her senses were still so disturbed, still so aware of how he made her feel when he kissed her.

The other half, even more worryingly, was urging her to wait, to delay, to busy herself with tasks that would keep her here in Stuart's home until the onset of dusk drove him inside.

Why? Because she was anxious to ensure that what had happened earlier was not going to have an adverse effect on their working relationship? Or because she wanted...needed physically and emotionally to see him, to be with him, to...?

Quickly she cut off her thoughts before they could encourage her down what caution warned her could be a very dangerous path.

Over supper she was so engrossed in her own thoughts that her mother had to address the same question to her several times before she heard it.

'I'm sorry,' she apologised. 'I was miles away.'

'Not missing London, are you, dear?' her mother asked her anxiously. 'We're enjoying having you here at home so much, but...'

'No, I'm not missing London at all,' Sara assured them, half surprised to realise how truthfully she had spoken. She had adapted to living and working here in the country far faster than she would have expected, had she ever actually stopped to contemplate the issue.

Of course every time she thought about Ian and Anna, and most especially about Anna's cruel revelations, she burned inwardly with pain and anguish, that pain as sharp as though someone had poured salt on an unhealed wound.

Only wasn't salt supposed to have a cleaning, cauterising effect on wounds—hadn't it once been a remedy for them?

Was the very sharpness of her pain somehow or other actually helping her to separate herself from the past? Was the thought of being somewhere where she might inadvertently come into contact with Ian and Anna so much an anathema to her that it made her revolt against the thought of returning to London?

But London was a very big place; the chances of her actually coming into contact with Ian and his fiancée were so remote...

So what was it that was keeping her here in Shropshire? The comfort and protection of her home...the warmth of her parents' love...the fact that she had a new and absorbing job?

Yes, all of these could contribute to her desire to stay, to prolong her sabbatical from her 'real' life, but none of them could surely be responsible for the deep atavistic thrill of fear-cum-rejection that had gripped her at the mere suggestion that she might want to return to London.

After all, London was the place where she had spent most of her adult life; where she had lived and worked very happily for the last decade. Was it purely because of Ian and Anna that she now found that the very last thing she wanted to do was to return there? After all, she had friends there, a pleasant social life, access to all manner of events that could not be catered for in a small rural environment.

Later on that night when she ought to have been asleep the question returned to vex her.

Outside the full moon beamed its light into her room through the curtains; she could hear the calls of the nocturnal creatures who like her seemed to be made restless by its subtle power. Why, when her mother had asked her if she wanted to return to London, had she experienced such intense revulsion...such sharp awareness of how much she dreaded the prospect and how little she wanted to return?

And why, when Stuart had kissed her, had she experienced all the emotions, all the vivid intense feelings which she had never experienced in Ian's arms?

Worrying questions to which she could not find any satisfactory or acceptable answers, questions which kept her awake and restless until well into the early hours of the morning.

CHAPTER SEVEN

STUART was avoiding her, Sara was sure of it. It was all very well for him to tell her that the sudden spell of exceptionally warm and dry weather meant that the nursery plantation in particular needed constant monitoring and attention; he still had to return to the house at some time or another. And yet no matter how early she arrived, or how late she stayed, ostensibly keeping on top of the greater volume of work arising from a sudden upsurge in demand for the trees, Stuart never seemed to be there.

It had been at her suggestion that he had placed additional advertising in several monthly magazines, including *Country Life*, and even she had been surprised at the volume of enquiries this advertising had brought.

Was it because of that kiss that they no longer shared those long and amazingly wide-ranging conversations she had enjoyed so much?

Miserably she acknowledged how much she was missing Stuart's company, and then, over a week after that highly charged scene, he walked into the office halfway through the afternoon, his face so set and strained that at first she imagined there had been some kind of accident.

She was halfway out of her chair, exclaiming anxiously, 'Stuart, what's wrong?' when he shook his head, telling her tersely,

'Nothing, it's just . . .' He stopped and turned his back on her, going to stand in front of the window, so that his body blocked out the light, turning the small study shadowy and somehow very intimate.

'There's something I want to say to you,' she heard him saying curtly. Her heart gave a frightened, anxious bound. Was he going to tell her that he didn't want her working for him any more? She could feel the pain, the despair the thought brought.

His back was still and set, his spine and his muscles tense. Her own body stiffened in response, in anticipation of what she had guessed he was about to say. She didn't want to listen to him, didn't want to hear him saying that he no longer needed her . . . didn't want to face up to the fact that, for whatever reason, he no longer wanted her in his life.

The friendship between them which had come to mean so much to her and which she had thought so well founded, so securely based, quite obviously was a total fiction, which she had created for herself and which could never have been as important to him as it was to her.

Her mouth had gone dry, her palms nervously sticky. Pride told her not to wait until he had said the actual words, but to anticipate him, to tell him she had guessed what it was he wanted to say, and that she quite agreed that it was time for her to leave . . . to return to her real life, but even as the words jostled for order in her brain, and she tried to get her tongue round them, he pre-empted her by asking brusquely, 'Did you mean it when you said that you'd be prepared to marry a man in order to have children?'

At first she was too stunned to speak, too stunned almost to even take in what he was saying. Her mind, her body, her emotions had been prepared for a far different question to this, and were not programmed as yet to deal competently with it.

His question had completely confused her, and it was several seconds before she could stammer, 'Well, yes ... yes, I did, but—— '

She wasn't allowed to continue; still without turning round Stuart interrupted her. 'Good. In that case I have a proposition to put to you.'

'A proposition?'

The bewilderment and confusion was clearly audible in her voice. Stuart turned round, the tension easing out of his face slightly, an almost rueful expression taking its place as he told her, 'Well, perhaps "proposal" would be a better word to use, although, being mindful of the romantic connotations of *that* particular word ... I'm asking you to marry me, Sara. Oh, I know this is probably neither the time nor the place; I can see how much I've shocked you, which does not bode well from my point of view, but I've been turning the whole thing over and over in my mind, trying to think of the best way to approach you, and in the end I decided that ... Well, suffice it to say that I decided the best approach was probably the most straight-forward one ...' He gave her a wry glance. 'I think John Senior thinks I'm off my head. We were just about to start planting out the new stock, when I suddenly knew I couldn't delay things any longer.

I've left him surrounded by damn near five hundred mixed saplings.'

Sara stared at him. She was, she discovered, shaking slightly, like someone caught up in the aftermath of a bad shock.

'You want to marry *me*? But——'

'I want a wife,' Stuart told her emotionlessly. 'Like you, I want a family, and it seems to me that since the two of us share so many interests, so many aims, plus the fact that we get on so well together, it must surely mean that a marriage between us must have at worst a fifty-per-cent chance of surviving and at best, given that such a marriage is something we both want and we're both prepared to commit ourselves to, a far higher chance of surviving than many marriages between two people who consider themselves to be in love and who also consider that that single emotion will be strong enough to bind them together for an entire lifetime.

'I'm not trying to pressure you, Sara; your reluctant acceptance isn't what I want, and, before you say anything, I have to admit that this is something I've been turning over in my mind for quite some time; that I've had time to become accustomed to the idea, to let it take root and grow, and, as it's grown, I've found myself coming to believe more and more firmly in it. You on the other hand haven't had any time as yet to do any of these things. I can see that I've surprised you . . . shocked you. Please don't reject the idea out of hand. Give yourself time to think about it. I'm quite prepared to wait. In the circumstances I wouldn't expect anything else than that you should need time to think it over ... perhaps even to discuss it with your family.'

'But we don't love one another,' Sara protested huskily. 'I ... You ...'

She was thinking as she spoke about that other woman. The woman he *had* loved. She was, she discovered, thinking about her, and wondering almost angrily if Stuart would have proposed to her if he hadn't suffered her rejection, which was surely an idiotic thing to do, especially in the circumstances; especially when she herself ...

Amazingly, instead of wanting to tell him immediately that there was no way she could even consider his proposal, never mind accept it, she discovered that her mind was flitting from one trivial aspect of the situation to another almost as though it was afraid to focus on the real nucleus of what had been suggested.

Marriage to Stuart ... Marriage to a man whom she didn't love ... Marriage to a man who did not love her ... It was a ridiculous suggestion, almost an insulting suggestion, and yet when her brain redirected the focus of the question and asked her how she felt about marriage to Stuart she was astonished to discover how easily and smoothly her emotions seemed to adapt to it. Marriage to Stuart ... children with Stuart ... Living here with Stuart and their children ...

Unconsciously her eyes registered her confused emotions. She realised that Stuart was watching her and flushed a little.

'It's ... It's ...'

'All so unexpected?' he asked her wryly.

'I ... I can't believe you mean it.'

'Take it from me, I do. In fact I've been nerving myself to discuss it with you since the first night we met.'

The night they'd met? But she hadn't told him about Margaret's advice that she should look round for a man whom she liked and with whom she could comfortably and compatibly live until the next day. She puzzled mentally over this for a few seconds and then realised that Stuart was still waiting for her to make some kind of response to his proposal... his proposition.

'I...I just don't know what to say,' she admitted helplessly.

'Does that mean you *do* know what to say, but don't want to offend me by doing so, or does it mean that you aren't entirely averse to the idea, but that you need rather more time to think it over?'

'Yes,' she told him, and then shook her head. 'I mean, no, I'm not averse to...to marrying you, but that I... Well...I wasn't expecting——'

'You mean, this is so sudden, Mr Delaney,' he interrupted her, lightening the mood by teasing her a little.

Sara laughed, grateful to him for injecting a little humour into the situation. 'Well, yes, it is,' she agreed. 'I mean, I know you——' She stopped, unwilling to say that she knew that he loved someone else, and that presumably that someone else, like Ian, was now forever out of his life. 'Well, I know that for both of us this marriage will be a sort of ''second-best'',' she amended hurriedly, unable to look at him, in case she saw in his eyes the pain caused by the knowledge that she was not really the one he wanted, the one he would have chosen, had he had the power of free choice.

To her surprise he checked her straight away, telling her almost curtly, 'I don't in any way see a marriage between us as being second-best; far from it. In fact in my view...' He stopped and then said more calmly, 'I've already said that I don't want to pressure you. I know what *I* want and I know that if you choose to marry me we'll have all the ingredients to make ourselves an extremely happy and enduring marriage, and a background for our children which will give them the best possible atmosphere in which to thrive and develop. Think about it, Sara. Obviously the sooner you feel able to give me your decision...

'At least we can be sure of one thing,' he added, turning away from her slightly. 'There can be no doubt that sexually we're going to be extremely compatible.'

How on earth did he know that? How on earth *could* he know it? She opened her mouth to ask him and then closed it again, conscious of a naïveté and self-consciousness that tied her tongue and kept her silent, while her pulse raced and a sensation like a tiny jolt of electricity burned through her body...an excitement...an awareness...an almost guilty knowledge of the way she had felt when he'd kissed her and how eagerly her senses had responded to him, how much she...

'I'd better get back to my saplings,' she heard Stuart saying behind her. 'If you wish you can call it a day and go home. I appreciate that I've hardly chosen the most appropriate circumstances in which to approach you, but——'

'No, no... After all, it isn't as though we're——'

'In love,' he supplied almost grimly for her. 'No, I suppose not. Even so, a little finesse...' He paused by the door and turned to look at her.

'No matter what you think now,' he told her quietly, 'as far as I'm concerned, a marriage between us would never come into the category of second-best. How you choose to view it is of course your own affair.'

He was gone before she could make any response.

Now that she was on her own, she felt rather as though she had fallen asleep and had a particularly vivid dream, but realistically she knew she had not been dreaming and that Stuart had in actual fact suggested to her that they might marry.

And yet what startled her most of all about the entire incident was not his proposal, but her own reaction to it, her own almost instinctive awareness of how easy it would have been to say yes, then and there... of how easy it was to contemplate the reality of being married to Stuart...

But he was right; it was something she needed to think through properly, to consider and then reconsider. Not just for her own sake. Not even for his, but, most importantly of all, for the children they both hoped they would have. She might be able to take the risk of making a mistake for her own sake, but not for theirs, never for theirs.

When she did as Stuart had suggested and went home she found her parents in the kitchen. Her mother was making pastry for a pie and her father was sitting in front of the range reading his newspaper.

'Sara, you're home early—is something wrong?' her mother asked anxiously as she walked in.

She shook her head, and then, a little to her own surprise, heard herself saying shakily, 'Stuart has just asked me to marry him.'

Later she told herself that she *had* intended to qualify her announcement, to explain that Stuart's proposal had been prompted not by love and passion but by logic and reason, but somehow or other in her mother's excited response to her news she found that by the time she had the opportunity to intercede and explain what had prompted his proposal it was too late because her parents had assumed that they were in love.

'Oh, but he's perfect for you,' her mother enthused. 'Just exactly the sort of man your father and I would have chosen. Have you set a date yet? When——?'

'Give her time to draw breath, Eileen,' her father protested mildly. 'Let the lass tell us herself what's happening.'

'We...we haven't made any firm plans yet,' Sara told them weakly. 'It's... it's early days, I haven't even——'

'Well, there's no reason for any delay,' her mother interrupted, before she could explain that she hadn't even accepted Stuart's proposal yet, or tell them what had prompted it. 'After all, you don't need to look for a house, or... You could have a June wedding. We could have the reception here in the garden. The roses will be at their best then, and the lawn's big enough for a marquee.'

Sara heard her father making a half-hearted protest about the potential hazard to his beloved garden, but she wasn't really listening. She was picturing herself wearing a misty creation of heavy old cream satin, floating ethereally toward Stuart while he . . .

She caught herself up with a guilty start. What on earth was she doing? She was far too sensible, and surely far too mature, to drift into that kind of daydream. Weddings . . . wedding dresses, the whole paraphernalia of a traditional ceremony had never really held any particular appeal to her, although by choice she would prefer a church ceremony, but as for the dress . . . She gave a small swallow of pain, surprised to discover how tight her throat was.

If she had been marrying Ian, he would either have wanted the brevity of a civil ceremony and no celebration or the exact opposite—an 'in' London church, the kind of reception that ran into thousands upon thousands of pounds, and hopefully made the gossip Press. From one extreme to the other, but then that was Ian: a man of extremes, of sudden passions and short-lived enthusiasms. Would he be faithful to Anna? If not, she would make him suffer for any infidelities. She was not the kind to suffer her pain in silence. Their marriage would be modern, bonded together by their mutual desire to live a fast-lane high-profile life.

As she contemplated the differences between the life she would have had married to Ian and the life she would have with Stuart, she acknowledged how painful and alien she would often have found her life with Ian. If he had loved her with the same intensity as she loved him, that would have com-

pensated for the lack of mutual goals...for the lack
of compatability. Or would it?

She gave a tiny shiver, causing her mother to ask
her anxiously if she was feeling all right.

'I'm fine,' she assured her.

'I must ring Jacqui. She'll be so thrilled. You'll
want to have the boys as pages, of course. Such a
pity Jessica is still only a baby.'

'Eileen,' Sara heard her father warn gruffly, 'this
is *Sara's* wedding. Give her a chance to say what
she wants, eh, love, before you go making all kinds
of plans? Don't fancy an elopement, do you, Sara?'
he asked teasingly, his expression hopeful.

Sara responded with a smile to this paternal
chestnut, while her mother protested, 'Good
heavens, Jack, what can you be suggesting? Of
course she doesn't. Of course there'll be a lot to
do...the catering for one thing, and the marquee.'

'Mum, I haven't...'

I haven't decided if I'm going to marry Stuart
yet, she had been going to say, but somehow or
other she found she had changed it to, 'I haven't
decided what kind of wedding to have yet. Stuart's
only just proposed. He might prefer something very
quiet and informal. Men do...'

'Well, maybe,' her mother allowed, 'but he'll
soon come round once he realises——'

'Eileen,' her father warned again, causing her
mother to stop, and say ruefully,

'I'm sorry, love. I *am* running on a bit, aren't I?
Of course it's up to you. If you'd rather have a
small wedding...'

'I'll have to discuss it with Stuart,' Sara told her.
She still couldn't believe it was all happening. Either

that Stuart had proposed or that she had somehow
or other allowed her mother to believe that not only
had she accepted him but also that their relationship and future marriage was not the prosaic
reality it actually was, but instead some kind of
romantic fantasy.

While she drank the cup of tea her mother had
poured her, she tried to come to terms with what
had happened. She would have to tell Stuart that
she wished to accept his proposal and soon,
otherwise the whole village would know that she
was marrying him before he did, she reflected wryly,
as she interrupted her mother's excited plans to
warn her that for the moment she wanted her news
to be kept between the four of them.

She tried to ring Stuart to suggest seeing him that
evening to explain to him what had happened and
to warn him that her parents now believed they were
madly in love, but as she had expected he wasn't
in. She would have to ring later when it had gone
dark or leave matters as they stood until the
morning.

The decision was taken out of her hands a little
later on over an early meal when her mother said,
'Well, I expect you'll be wanting to get changed
and get back to Stuart. No doubt we'll hardly see
anything of you between now and the wedding. I
remember how it was when your father and I were
engaged ... Couldn't spend enough time together,
could we, Jack?'

It was no use now trying to explain to her parents
that their relationship was completely different from
the one she would be having with Stuart and that,
far from wanting to spend every possible second

with her, he would probably appreciate a little distance.

She frowned to herself as she tried to work out why that knowledge should cause her a pain like a tiny sliver of ice embedding itself in her heart.

She delayed for as long as she could before giving in to her mother's urging to go upstairs and get ready to drive back to the manor.

When she came downstairs, having changed into a clean shirt, still wearing the suit she had worn for work, her mother expostulated with her that she might have chosen to wear something a little more feminine and pretty.

A shadow touched her eyes as she turned away from her, her mild criticism suddenly far too reminiscent of Anna's taunts.

Was she unfeminine? She had never thought so; perhaps her clothes were a little on the formal, businesslike side, but she felt equally at home in her jeans, a thick sweater and a pair of Wellington boots. If she chose not to wear frills and fussy flounces, surely that did not rob her of her femininity.

'Leave the lass alone,' she heard her father saying easily. 'She looks fine the way she is.'

'Of course you do,' her mother reassured her. 'I just thought . . .'

Quietly Sara opened the kitchen door. She was committed now; it was too late for second thoughts and all because she had allowed her mother to jump to the wrong conclusion, thus forcing her into an acceptance of Stuart's proposal, his 'proposition', as he had termed it. And yet hadn't she known deep inside herself what would happen the moment she tried to explain the situation to her mother? Had she done so in fact with a hidden secret corner of her mind already knowing what the outcome would be?

After all, wasn't it far easier to tell herself that she had had no option but to accept Stuart's proposal, once her mother had assumed they were in love, than to coldbloodedly and analytically weigh up the fors and againsts of the situation like two opposing columns of figures?

Despite all her doubts, all her awareness of how very unorthodox what she was doing was, she now *wanted* to marry Stuart and yet until he had broached the subject it had never even occurred to her.

It surprised her how quickly, how easily she had come to envisage herself in the role of his wife.

He would not be expecting her to return this evening. He might even be out, she warned herself as she drove up the lane and then parked in front of the house.

Now that she was here, she felt a little uncomfortable, a little foolish and very, very vulnerable. After all, what she had to say to him could quite easily have waited until the morning. She could surely have easily found some way of deflecting her mother's curiosity at the fact that they weren't spending the evening together; told her that Stuart was under pressure to complete his new planting.

There was no sign of the Land Rover in the yard as she stopped, just a pile of what looked like huge old pieces of wood. Stuart was obviously still working, which meant that she would either have to return home, stay here and hope that he came back soon, or drive over the estate looking for him.

Rejecting the latter course, she was just mulling over what she should do when she heard the Land Rover approaching the house.

'Sara!' Stuart hailed her as he cut the engine and got out. 'I wasn't expecting...'

'No, I know, but my mother...' Realising she was beginning her explanation from the wrong end, Sara stopped, took a deep breath and then asked him unsteadily, 'Stuart, was I dreaming this afternoon or did you really suggest that we should get married?'

'You weren't dreaming,' he assured her, watching her.

In the strident light from the security lights illuminating the yard he looked tired. There were streaks of dirt on his face, and a small laceration on his cheekbone where a thin whippy branch had perhaps cut the flesh.

As he came towards her, she caught the warm, active scent of his skin and to her consternation she felt her body reacting overwhelmingly to it.

Thank goodness she wasn't actually wearing the soft feminine frills suggested by her mother was her first panicky thought. Had she been, the swelling tautness of her nipples would have been instantly visible to anyone who looked at her, including Stuart himself.

As it was she had to suppress a sharp urge to pull her jacket more protectively around her body, conscious as she moved that even the small friction caused by that movement caused her now sensitive nipples to throb and ache.

'Let's get inside,' she heard Stuart saying. 'You're obviously cold.'

Her face flamed as she thought that he must somehow after all have noticed what had happened to her, and then she realised that it was far more likely to be the fact that she was hugging herself into her jacket that made him think she was chilled.

As she followed him inside, she protested, 'I shouldn't really be here. You probably haven't even eaten yet, and I know how busy you are...'

'Not too busy to make time for you,' he assured her, turning to give her a grave-eyed look. 'Something's obviously worrying you. I take it you've discussed my... my proposition with your parents.'

'Well, I tried to, only Mum got the wrong end of the stick and before I could stop her she'd assumed that it was more of a proposal than a proposition. She thinks that you and I are in love,' she told him starkly. 'I know I ought to have at least tried to explain to her, but once she'd made the assumption, and was obviously thrilled with the idea...' She gave a helpless shrug.

'It's cowardly of me, I know. I *should* have told her the truth, but it would be rather like trying to stop an express train,' she told him ruefully. 'Before we'd even finished our cup of tea, she'd virtually got the wedding planned. A marquee on the lawn— a June wedding... Oh, I'm so sorry, Stuart; you must think me very weak-minded. I didn't intend to come up here like this when I know how busy you are, but Mum had virtually pushed me out of the house before I could stop her. She even told me she thought I ought to change into something more feminine.'

She stopped as she heard Stuart laugh.

'You're not . . . you're not annoyed, then?' she asked him uncertainly.

'Not if your mother's very natural misconception means that you *are* going to marry me.'

Sara ignored the fierce leap of sensation his words caused inside her, and concentrated instead on anxiously trying to make sure he fully understood what had happened.

'She'll expect us to behave as though we're in love. I don't know if you realise . . .'

'Well, of course she will, and so will everyone else, but I don't see that being any problem. After all, I don't know about you, but I hadn't intended to go round telling everyone that ours was a marriage founded on . . . on mutual beliefs and aims, rather than on mutual passion. The reasons for our marriage are our affair and need not concern anyone else.'

'But you don't understand,' Sara protested helplessly. 'People will expect——'

'People will expect what? Us to behave like lovers? I think your mother's right. I think a June wedding will be ideal.'

When she frowned and looked confused, he explained quietly, 'June is less than six weeks away. The sooner we get married, and settle down to the mundanity of married life, the faster people will cease regarding our relationship as a novelty, putting it under a microscope, so to speak. I don't think it's a task beyond either of us to at least give some semblance of being idyllically happy together in public for the short space of six weeks, do you?

That is, of course, if you have decided that marriage to me *is* what you want.'

'What? Oh, yes, it is...that is, I do...' Sara told him in a flustered voice. Married in June. So soon... She felt a tiny flutter of nerves beat frantic wings inside her stomach.

'Why don't you stay and have supper with me?' Stuart suggested. 'We can talk the whole thing over then.'

Immediately she shook her head. Not because she didn't want to be with him, but because as yet the whole situation was still too new to her, and because her body, that rebellious entity which seemed to be behaving in such an uncharacteristic way recently, was something she couldn't trust in its present mood. Witness the way it had already reacted to him once this evening.

'No, no, I must get back,' she fibbed, edging her way towards the door.

For a moment he looked oddly grim, unfamiliar almost, a different Stuart from the one she knew, and then he was striding past her to open the door for her and to walk with her to her car.

As she passed the collection of wood by the door, she asked him curiously, 'What on earth's that?'

'Pieces of oak I rescued from a demolition site.'

'Oh, you mean like the wood you used for the kitchen units?' she asked him, enlightenment dawning.

'That's right,' he agreed, without specifying what purpose he intended to put it to.

Outside her car, she hesitated, telling herself she had no right at all to feel chagrined or rejected when he made no move to touch her or kiss her, and yet oddly enough as she drove home she did feel conscious of a small ache, not just of disappointment but of apprehension as well. They would be sexually compatible, he had said, and yet how could he really know that on the strength of one or two kisses? It was all very well for them both to talk logically and calmly of their mutual desire to have children, to be parents, but what if when the time came...?

She trembled a little, clutching the steering-wheel of her car. It was too late to have those kind of thoughts now. She was committed. There was no going back.

Committed. Wasn't that how they'd used to describe people who were locked away in those awful Victorian mental institutions? Committed...

She gave another tiny shiver. *Was* she mad to have accepted Stuart's proposal? Would a marriage between them work? Would it endure? Would they be able to build a secure, happy environment for their children?

Beneath her apprehensive fear, she was conscious of a slow, steady pulse of calming reassurance; a deep-seated and deeply buried belief that if she would just allow herself to ignore her fears she would find it surprisingly easy to accept that she had done the right thing.

At the moment she was allowing her judgement to be clouded by the mythology that surrounded modern courtship and marriage: the belief that only the most intense and passionate of emotions could be any basis for marriage. She must put aside that conditioning, that reasoning, which was after all no reasoning at all. She must turn her thoughts away from the past and towards the future; a future which she owed it to Stuart to commit herself to completely.

Commit . . . there was that word again. She must make the same commitment to Stuart that he was obviously prepared to make to her. Now suddenly she found the word comforting rather than frightening.

Commitment. Yes, she liked the sound of that, and she must not forget that Stuart, like her, knew already what it was like to experience all the pain of loving the wrong person, and of not having that love returned. They had so much in common; far more than she had ever had with Ian.

They *could* be happy; it was after all up to them.

CHAPTER EIGHT

THEY could be happy. Sara soon discovered how prophetic that thought had been.

Well as she had thought she had known Stuart, it had surprised her to discover what a good actor he was, and how easily and convincingly he slipped into the role of a man on the verge of marriage to a woman with whom he was very much in love on those occasions when they had to appear together in public as a prospective bridal couple.

There had been Sunday lunch with her family, arranged so that her sister, her husband and the children could be with them; a visit to the vicar to arrange the dates for the ceremony. Stuart, it seemed, shared her mother's view that since they were going to get married they might as well do so in style, thus endearing him even more to her parents; and, making him even more popular with her father, he had tactfully suggested that since the manor had much larger grounds and a far less well-cared-for garden it might be as well to have the marquee and the reception there.

They weren't having a formal engagement; there was no point when they were getting married so quickly. Everyone who knew them both, or so it seemed, was now announcing that they had felt all along that they were an ideal couple, something which caused Stuart to give her a wryly amused glance whenever this view was uttered.

He *would* make a wonderful father, Sara had acknowledged, watching him with her sister's children; he was patient, caring, concerned...everything that any woman could want in her life's partner, and yet she was still afraid.

Not of wishing that she had not married him...not even of discovering that no matter how much she liked him he could never take the place she had reserved for so long for Ian.

No, surprisingly enough what she feared was disappointing him—waking up one morning and discovering that he had changed his mind...or, even worse, waking up one morning after they were married to discover that, as Anna had predicted, sexually *she* was so unappealing, so undesirable that he could no longer bring himself to touch her.

And because of the intimacy of her fears, and the revelations which must automatically accompany them, she was afraid to voice them.

She knew that had she had enough previous sexual experience she would not be suffering this anxiety; that if she could look back over her life and say mentally to herself, maybe *Ian* didn't want me, but there were others—or even one other—it would be different, but because of her nature she had never felt inclined to experiment sexually, and, no matter how much she might regret this now, there was no way she could turn back the clock and alter things.

She was twenty-nine years old and still a virgin, and she was terrified that when she and Stuart eventually came together as man and wife he would find her so undesirable that their marriage would be destroyed.

A woman was designed by nature to accept a man's sexual advances, even though she might not feel intense desire for him, but a man...

Her fear worried at her mind without cessation—the only person she felt she could discuss it honestly and openly with was Margaret.

She rang her one afternoon when she had the office to herself.

'Sara!' her friend exclaimed when she answered the phone. 'How are you? Only three weeks to go now. By the way, guess what—I'm pregnant. Some surprise, eh?'

Margaret pregnant—the sharp pang of envy that engulfed her body confirmed to Sara, if she needed any confirmation, just how committed she now was to the concept of marriage to Stuart. They had already discussed the subject of their future children. Stuart wanted to wait until they had been married for six months before they started their family, and she had agreed. Now suddenly she felt an impulsive aching urgency to have conceived already. Because she wanted a child, or because it would tie Stuart more firmly to her?

She was so shocked that she should even consider such a course that for a moment she couldn't speak.

'Sara, are you still there?' Margaret demanded.

'Yes, yes. I'm here. I'm thrilled about the baby... Thrilled and envious.'

Margaret laughed. 'Well, it will soon be your turn.'

'I hope so... Margaret, there's something I need to discuss with you.'

Her voice sharpened with anxiety and tension, causing the laughter to drop from her friend's voice as she questioned, 'What's wrong? Not having second thoughts, are you? Both Ben and I think Stuart is ideal for you. If you're still thinking about Ian——'

'No, no, it isn't that. I *want* to marry Stuart. It's just...' She paused, and then said quickly, 'With you and Ben... Did you...? Well, I know you said you weren't in love with him. But sexually...' She paused, unable to go on.

'I think I know what you're asking me,' Margaret told her gently. 'There'd been other men before Ben, and naturally neither of us would have contemplated committing ourselves to marriage if we hadn't at least made sure that we *could* be sexually intimate, but if you're at all worried that you don't find Stuart sexually desirable——'

'No. No, it isn't that,' Sara interrupted her, gulping nervously, as she rushed on before she could lose her courage, 'I know it's ridiculous in this day and age, but there hasn't been anyone else for me, and I'm afraid... well, I'm afraid that Stuart is going to find me a disappointment. That I won't...that he won't...'

There was a pause and then Margaret asked her slowly, 'Have you told him any of this? Discussed your fears?'

'No. No, I haven't...I——'

'Then you must,' Margaret told her firmly.

When she made no response, Margaret added gently, 'You're going to marry the man, Sara—if you can't even bring yourself to tell him how you feel, how on earth are you going to...? And besides,

think of his feelings. You're a virgin. He ought to
know that. If you can't bring yourself to tell him,
then why don't you write him a note? Explain...'

'When shall I give it to him?' Sara asked her
grimly. 'Halfway through the wedding ceremony?
And as for telling him... what am I supposed to
say? "Oh, by the way, I haven't mentioned it
before, but I'm actually still a virgin?" He'll think
there's something wrong with me. He'll think——'

'Don't be ridiculous,' Margaret chided her. 'He
won't think anything of the sort. In fact, if you
want my opinion——' She broke off. 'Oh, hell, I've
got to go. Alan's just come in. Paul has fallen off
the swing and cut his head. Look, Sara, tell him.
Tell him... Now! Today. I suspect you're worrying
about it far more than he will. He isn't Ian, you
know,' she added before hanging up.

Tell him. Tell Stuart that she wasn't coming to
him with all the benefit of being sexually experienced and at ease, and yet oddly enough, as she sat
staring into space, she suddenly realised that given
the choice between the two men the one she would
have automatically chosen as her first lover wasn't
Ian.

Ian. It surprised her sometimes how difficult she
found it even to recall his face, and yet not so very
long ago he had been her whole world.

She still ached inside whenever she recalled her
conversation with Anna and she suspected she
always would. The wounds the other woman had
inflicted could never heal; weren't they after all part
of the reason for her fear now?

Tell him, Margaret had urged her. And yet how
could she? In public he played the role of the loving

fiancé to perfection, but in private... In private he never touched her, never gave her the slightest indication that he found her desirable, that he wanted her—but then why should he?

But they were going to be married. They were going to have children. Her panic swelled inside her, tightening her muscles, making her head and back ache with tension.

Stuart was away for the whole day, delivering an order. He had told her that he didn't expect to be back until late in the evening.

He had been kind to her over these last three weeks of their engagement, but distant, never coming to stand beside her or lean over her shoulder as she worked as he had done before they had decided to get married.

She was shocked by how much she missed this most casual of physical contact with him. She was like someone who was secretly starving, she told herself with distaste, someone so desperate for physical affection...any kind of physical affection. And yet why should she be like this? In the ten years she had known Ian, she had never suffered any awareness of this kind of deprivation. She had loved Ian, yes, had longed for him to kiss her, to make love to her, but with hindsight she recognised that that longing had been based on a confused belief that if he did so it would mean that he must care for her, whereas with Stuart... With Stuart she actually physically ached for *him* to touch her, actually had to physically stop herself from moving closer to him.

She had already noticed that when they were out together in public she automatically closed the distance between them, walking as close to his side as it was possible for her to get, until she realised what she was doing and forced herself to move away from him.

She wasn't completely naïve. She knew quite well that it was possible to experience desire without love, but before she had always imagined that that was more a male experience, and she had certainly never suspected that she would ever experience such a sharply painful need.

She wanted Stuart as her lover, she acknowledged with a tiny shiver, which surely could only bode well for their marriage, and yet...

What if the very intensity of her wanting should repel him, drive them apart? She tried to envisage how she would feel were their positions reversed: if he wanted her, and she could only accept him because of her desire to have children. Wouldn't *she* in those circumstances feel overwhelmed, threatened, angered, and finally completely turned off by the sheer intensity of his desire?

She got up and moved restlessly around the room, hugging her arms around her body. She had lost weight recently; her mother had remarked on it when they went to buy her wedding dress in Ludlow. Nothing in the shop had appealed until the girl had suddenly produced a dress in heavy cream satin, its style vaguely Tudorish, showing off the cream embroidery on the fabric. She had touched it, had had a vision of herself gliding down the main staircase at the manor, and she had known then that the dress was just what she had been looking for.

It had unfortunately needed altering, but the girl had promised her that it would be ready in plenty of time. She was due to go for a fitting the week before the wedding. Her mother was determinedly trying to feed her up, telling her that she must not lose any more weight, otherwise it wouldn't fit.

The strain was telling on both of them. There had been several occasions when she had caught Stuart watching her almost broodingly.

She had longed to ask him if he was having second thoughts and yet at the same time had been afraid to do so. What if he said he was? She tried to tell herself that if he asked to be released from their agreement it would probably be for the best; that it was not after all as though their emotions were involved; that he had every right to change his mind; and yet the thought of his doing so caused her such fear and pain.

Had Anna's taunts traumatised her so much that she now expected and dreaded rejection in any form? Had it made her feel so vulnerable, so insecure as a woman?

Her head was pounding and she felt slightly sick. She stared at the VDU and found she was unable to focus properly on it. She hadn't been sleeping well. There was so much to do, not just here in the office but with the arrangements for the wedding, with the work on the house, which Stuart had brought forward because he felt that, while the house was comfortable enough as it was for a bachelor, she, as a woman, needed more comfort, more luxury.

She had tried to protest, telling him that it was not necessary for him to go to such lengths, but he had overruled her, and for the last three weeks the house had been filled with the noisy clatter of workmen brought in to repair the plasterwork in the small sitting-room, and to redecorate it, and to do the same in the large panelled room that was the master bedroom, and the bathroom adjoining it.

Originally, she recognised, those two adjoining rooms must have been 'his and hers' bedrooms, and she had been half tempted to ask him if in the circumstances he might not prefer to revert to their traditional usage.

Today the workmen had left early. The repaired plasterwork needed to dry out before the redecoration could start.

She had spent the last few evenings poring over a variety of books and catalogues, searching for authentic period room illustrations to give her some guidelines on which to choose the décor and furnishings of the newly repaired rooms.

She had already mentioned wistfully to Stuart that the bedroom with its fine panelling and huge renovated fireplace called out for an equally large oak four-poster bed, but she had seen the cost of such beds in the catalogues she had obtained, and they ran into thousands rather than hundreds of pounds, and that was without the heavy damask curtains, the antique crewelwork covers, the expensive Turkey rugs, and the other furniture the room would need to bring it properly to life.

Much as she loved the house and was looking forward to living in it, she had to admit that things would have been considerably simpler if it had just been a comfortably sized modern house they were furnishing.

Stuart had suggested that it might be best if she avoided going near the upstairs rooms while the men were working on them, because of the danger of damaged falling plaster, and she had taken his hint and kept well out of their way.

The pounding in her head increased. She still had work to finish but the afternoon sun pouring in through the window was making her feel sick and dizzy. Perhaps if she went home and took a couple of tablets the headache might clear, enabling her to come back and finish her work early in the evening when the sun would no longer be shining in through this particular window.

With a faint sigh of exasperation for her own weakness, she got up and collected her things.

Luckily when she got home she discovered that her parents were out, enabling her to take a couple of tablets and go straight upstairs to bed.

Much as she loved them both, this was one occasion on which the last thing she wanted was company...and the second last was to discuss the wedding.

When she woke up she could tell from the coolness of her room that she had been asleep for several hours. She moved cautiously and then acknowledged with relief that her headache had gone.

She got up, stripped off her clothes, and showered quickly before redressing, this time more casually, in clean underwear topped by a pair of faded old jeans and a chunky cotton-knit sweater with a design in pastels on a white background which her sister had bought her for her birthday the previous summer.

When she went downstairs her parents were watching television. Her mother made to get up, but she stopped her.

'Sorry I missed supper,' she apologised. 'I had the most awful headache, so I came home early and went straight to bed. I've got to go back, though. I've got some work I must finish.'

'I'll make you a drink first, and something to eat,' her mother announced, starting to get up, but Sara shook her head.

'Oh, no, you won't. You stay right where you are. I'll make us all a drink and I'll have a quick snack, but it's gone eight now, and I've at least a couple of hours' work left.'

'Will you wait for Stuart to get back?' her mother asked her.

'I might, although he said it would be very late.' At the back of her mind lay the knowledge that Margaret had been right to urge her to talk to Stuart about her fears, and her conversation with her friend had highlighted a point she herself had not previously considered: that being that Stuart might feel that, in not being honest and open with him in the first place, she had placed an additional burden on the wrong side of the scales weighing out the success or otherwise of their marriage.

The rear of the house was in darkness as she drove up to it, the security lights coming on as she parked her car. She got out and unlocked the back door with the keys Stuart had given her, switching on the lights as she made her way to the study.

She had just settled herself down and switched on the computer terminal when she thought she heard a noise coming from upstairs.

She froze, switching off the machine, her ears straining as she listened, but now she could hear nothing.

Telling herself she must be imagining things, she was about to switch on the machine again and start work, when she decided instead that it might be as well to go upstairs and check. And besides, now that the workmen had finished it would surely be safe for her to look inside the rooms on which they had been working.

Inwardly acknowledging that the noise she thought she had heard was probably just an excuse to exorcise her curiosity, she headed for the stairs.

If she had heard anything, she decided as she walked up them, it must simply have been the house settling down for the night, because she could hear nothing now.

She had used the back stairs, remembering Stuart's wry comment that it was going to cost a fortune to carpet the place, walking quickly along the broad gallery off which opened the main bedrooms.

The gallery overlooked the formal gardens to what had originally been the front of the house, but was now the side. It had small paned casement windows which were bowed in places, the glass thick, and, like the leading, original. Beneath the windows were window-seats, where presumably the ladies of the house, weary of promenading along the gallery, could sit to stare down into the gardens below.

The polished floorboards were the original oak: wide, and dusty from the toing and froings of the workmen, but once polished...

Sara smiled wryly to herself; already she was becoming very much the housewife, the châtelaine, although she had no illusions about the sacrifices both in money and in time that such a house would demand.

Ultimately, though, it would be worthwhile. She smiled to herself, wondering how she would cope with the hazard of small tricycles being pedalled up and down her polished floors on wet days, and she was still smiling as she pushed open the door to the main bedroom.

'Sara...'

She froze as Stuart said her name, staring at him in shocked astonishment. He was kneeling on the floor beside the most beautifully carved oak tester bed she had ever seen, meticulously rubbing wax into the carvings.

'Stuart! I had no idea... I thought you were still out. I was working downstairs. I heard a noise...'

She was gabbling, she recognised, as she struggled with a mingled sense of shock and guilt.

'I managed to get back earlier than I anticipated.'

'But I didn't see the Land Rover.'

'No. It developed a small problem with the petrol pump so I dropped it off at the garage and got them to give me a lift back. You say you came back to work?' He was frowning.

'Yes. I left early this afternoon. I had a headache, but there was something I wanted to finish.'

'That makes two of us,' he commented, as he stood up and stretched.

Helplessly she followed the movement, hearing the faint crack of his muscles, watching the way the soft fabric of his worn denim shirt moulded itself to his body. There was an ache in the pit of her stomach; a tension in her body that made her muscles tremble slightly. She felt dizzy, confused by her own feelings... her own desires.

'The bed,' she said huskily. 'It's beautiful, but they're so expensive...'

'This one wasn't,' he told her mildly. 'At least not in terms of money. I admit there've been occasions over the past three weeks when I have wondered if I'd bitten off more than I could chew. Generally around one o'clock in the morning.'

He said it so drily that it was several seconds before she realised what he meant.

'You... you made it,' she exclaimed in awe. 'But how?'

'Remember the wood you saw outside?'

She nodded, and then said, 'But the carving... it's so intricate, so...'

She moved closer to the bed, reaching out to touch one of the panels, unable to resist stroking her fingers over its surface. Stuart had carved a frieze of trees and flowers on the base and head-boards, and the outside of the wooden over-canopy was carved in a traditional form of relief-work.

'Stuart, it's beautiful,' she told him shakily.

'You weren't supposed to see it, at least not yet,' he told her severely. 'It was *supposed* to be my wedding present for you.'

'You did *this* for *me*?'

She turned from the bed to look at him. For some reason she felt shockingly close to tears, her emotions far too close to the surface.

She could feel the tears filling her eyes, blurring her vision.

She started to look away but it was too late. Stuart was coming towards her, exclaiming curtly, 'Sara...what *is* it? What's *wrong*? Have you changed you mind? Would you...?'

She shook her head.

'No, not that...'

'But *something's* wrong,' he insisted.

'Not wrong,' she denied, shaking her head. 'It's just...'

Her hand touched the mattress. The bed was high and took two deep mattresses. Lying inside, it would be like being on a very private, very secret island, she reflected.

'It's just that what?' Stuart pressed.

He was, she realised, still standing very close to her. So close that when she turned her head she could feel the warmth of his breath brushing her skin.

'Is it this that bothers you, Sara?' he asked her quietly, his hand joining hers on the mattress. She focused on their hands; symbolically they were separate...apart...his hard and tanned, his nails clean and short, hers smaller, paler, her nails free of colour but somehow undeniably feminine and delicate in a way she hadn't noticed before. Certainly they were nothing like Anna's hands with their long polished nails, just as Stuart's weren't like Ian's with their careful manicure and buffed sheen. Ian was a vain man . . . an almost effeminate man in some ways perhaps.

'Are you worrying that when you share this bed with me it will be a poor substitute for what you had with him? Because——'

'No . . . No . . . It's nothing like that,' she denied frantically, and then when he stopped and waited she blurted out, 'There never was anything like that between me and Ian. In fact . . .' She paused, and then before she could change her mind she rushed ahead, telling him with defiant anguish, 'In fact, there hasn't been anything like that with . . . with anyone . . .'

She couldn't bear to look at him. The tears were really blurring her eyes now. She tried to blink them away and focus on the bed. She was, she discovered with detached curiosity, actually physically trembling.

She felt Stuart's hand on her hair, his touch somehow soothing, comforting, warming her chilled tense muscles, even though her throat still ached with the effort of suppressing her tears.

His hand slid to her jaw, cupping her face, turning her towards him. But she still couldn't bring herself to look at him, even though she knew he was watching her.

'And you're afraid,' he asked her gently, gesturing towards the bed as he added quietly. 'Afraid of all that this represents, because it is unknown, unfamiliar.'

He seemed so calm, so understanding . . . so . . . so comforting.

She nodded and gulped. 'Yes.' Heavens, she was behaving like a complete fool. If he still wanted to marry her after this...

He was silent for so long that she started to tremble again. His hand was still cupping her face. Now his thumb stroked her skin almost absently and then he said softly, 'There really isn't anything to fear. I promise you it's all going to be all right.'

She wanted to tell him that her fear was not of him, or even of the intimacies they would share, but of disappointing him, of ultimately being rejected by him when he discovered that she simply wasn't woman enough to make their marriage worthwhile and well founded, but, before she could find the courage to do so, astoundingly, she heard him saying slowly, 'Here, let me show you.'

CHAPTER NINE

Show her.

Now she did look at him, her head jerking upwards, her eyes wide with confusion and shock, her sudden movement causing his thumb to press firmly against the corner of her mouth.

Whether because of that pressure, or whether because of her own shock, she wasn't sure, but her lips parted, her tongue-tip touching them in nervous apprehension.

He was going to kiss her. Already he was lowering his head towards hers. She looked wildly into his eyes and then away, conscious of how dizzy the steadiness of his gaze was making her feel. She focused on his mouth instead, but that was even more of a mistake. Her heart started to hammer and trip with frantic haste; she made a small instinctive sound of protest ... but made no effort to resist him when he took her in his arms.

He had kissed her before, so she should have known what to expect, but somehow this time the effect on her senses was even more intense, even more shockingly erotic, her lips parting helplessly, eagerly almost beneath the warm moist pressure of his.

She heard the sound he made against her mouth and her body trembled in response, logic and rationality put to flight by the storm of sensation sweeping through her.

She could feel Stuart's hands on her body, smoothing down over her back, encircling her waist as he urged her closer to him, so close in fact that her breasts were pressed flat against him. Her legs started to tremble as she became engulfed by his heat and scent. She made a small helpless sound beneath his mouth and instantly the pressure of his kiss changed, softening, deepening as though she had called out a message to him and he had responded to it.

His hands moved back up over her body, tangling in her hair as they spread against her scalp, holding her a willing captive.

He said her name, breathing it into her mouth with a kind of hungry urgency that made her body quiver.

He was kissing her less intensely now, biting gently at her mouth, his fingers moving against her scalp like a cat's paws weaving, the motion relaxing... soothing.

He was also, she realised, easing himself away from her body. She wanted to protest, to tell him how much she now needed the heat and power of him against her, but it was impossible for her to voice such words, and so instead she clung silently to him, her fingers curling into the solid muscles of his upper arms, her eyes huge and dazed, her mouth softly bruised from his kiss.

He lifted one hand from her head, his body flexing slightly in a gesture of gentle denial, and then as she started to shrink back from him, her eyes registering her pain, he said rawly, 'Sara...No...You don't...'

Her mouth started to tremble. Stuart made a sound deep in his throat. His hand touched her face; his thumb stroked gently against her swollen bottom lip.

The heat that shot through her made her cry out loud in shocked panic, her lips parted, and Stuart's thumb slipped inside the moist warmth of her mouth.

She touched it with her tongue-tip, an automatic and instinctive reaction. The texture of his skin felt rough, and tasted slightly salty. She licked it again, surprised to discover how pleasurable it was. She closed her eyes and made a soft sound of pleasure, sucking experimentally on his thumb, and finding the sensation so addictive that it took Stuart's fierce shudder, and the explosive sound of denial he made as he called out her name protestingly, to make her realise what she was doing.

'Sara!'

She released his thumb and stared helplessly at him, guilty colour flooding her face as he cupped it, this thumb making a damp imprint against her skin.

'You haven't any idea what you're doing to me, have you?' he asked her, his voice softening slightly. 'You haven't any idea how much you're...you're turning me on...making me want you.'

Her shock showed in her eyes.

'You don't believe me, do you? Let me show you.'

He was unfastening the buttons of his shirt, pulling it out of his jeans. His torso was tanned and firmly muscled. A line of soft dark hair angled downwards, disappearing beneath his belt.

Her mouth had gone very dry, but her pulses were racing, and it wasn't fear she felt when he took her hand and placed it on his chest against his heart.

Her eyes widened as she registered its frantic fierce beat. She lifted her gaze to his face and saw that there was an unfamiliar flush of colour burning up under his skin, that his eyes looked darker...that they were glittering in a way that made her own body react as immediately and as physically as though he had actually touched it.

Beneath her sweater her breasts swelled and ached. Guiltily she looked away from him. He was breathing raggedly, the muscles in his throat tense, his skin slightly damp. She wondered whether, if she licked it, it would taste the same as his thumb. She could feel her own breath constricting in her throat. She tried to look away but couldn't, helplessly captivated by the irregular rise and fall of his chest.

Was his body like hers, filled with heated excitement at the thought of being touched, being caressed? Did he long for her hands, her mouth against him as much as she...?

'You see,' she heard him saying roughly. And then he was lifting her hand towards his mouth, his thumb caressing the pulse in her wrist, and, before she realised what he intended to do, he was caressing her fingers with his tongue, slowly, tantalisingly licking and sucking them while her heart turned over inside her and the heat she had felt before was nothing compared with the sheet of burning, exquisite agony and need that ripped through her now. She actually thought for a moment that she was going to faint, and it seemed that Stuart thought so too, because he released her hand and caught hold of her, picking her up off the floor and holding her tightly, comfortingly, rocking her slightly as though he knew how ill-equipped she was to deal with the sensations he had aroused.

She was shaking so much that she was afraid if he put her down she wouldn't actually be able to stand, but he showed no inclination to put her fear to the test.

His hands were resting on her skin beneath her sweater, their touch firm...comforting.

'I ought to stop this right now before it all gets out of hand,' she heard him murmuring against her ear. 'But somehow I don't think I'm going to be able to.' He gave a small sigh, and she wondered achingly if he already knew how little she wanted him to stop, how much she...

'Do you know what I want right now?' he whispered to her. 'I want to take off your clothes, and lie here with you, your body against mine, your skin caressing mine. I want to kiss you and hold you...to stroke you and love you. And I want those things more than I've ever wanted anything before in my life.'

It wasn't true, of course, it couldn't *be* true, because after all, as she already knew, he loved someone else, but the words were like a magical salve, soothing and healing the wounds Anna had inflicted.

She wasn't conscious of saying anything, or doing anything in response to what he had told her, but there must have been something, some softening of her body, some secret subtle message which passed between her flesh and his, because the next minute he was kissing her, not quite as gently as he had done before, his body moving urgently and erotically against her own, his hands caressing her back beneath her sweater, hesitating when they reached the barrier of her bra, pausing for a second and then unclipping it so that the fragile silk of her bra fell away, and when he moved the rough abrasion of her cotton-knit sweater against the sensitive arousal of her breasts was a stimulation that made her want to cry out to him to touch her there, to stroke her, to kiss her.

She trembled beneath the tempest of sensations assailing her, making a small sharp sound of bewilderment that caused Stuart to break off his kiss and murmur against her mouth, 'Ssh... It's all right... Everything's all right.'

Only it wasn't. She ached so badly inside; wanted him so much, yearned to reach out and touch his skin, to explore and caress his body with an intensity she had never imagined she could ever feel.

She tried to tell him, struggling to formulate the words, to get him to stop what he was doing right now before she embarrassed him and humiliated herself, but before she could get any further than 'I want...' he was easing her out of her sweater and then her jeans, picking her up, kissing her with a slow tenderness that made her forget everything other than her need to respond to him.

When he stepped back from her to remove his own clothes, she was trembling so much that she had to sit down, perching on the edge of the bed, hardly able to comprehend that this was actually happening; that Stuart was actually making love to her...that he actually seemed to want her...to desire her.

She shivered again, suddenly self-conscious and nervous, causing Stuart to kneel down at her side.

Without his clothes his body was taut and strong-muscled, narrow-hipped and flat-buttocked in contrast to her own softer curves.

His hand touched her knee in a brief gesture of reassurance and comfort.

'It's all right,' he told her quietly. 'Everything's going to be all right, and I promise you that if you...if you want me to stop, I shall.'

If she wanted him to stop. She shivered, wondering what he would say if she were to tell him that that was the last thing she wanted. She bent her head, so that her hair swung forward to conceal her expression from him.

His head, she realised, was on a level with her breasts.

She wondered if they looked as swollen and tautly eager for his touch to him as they did to her, shamelessly flaunting their desire.

He lifted his hand, gently cupping their silken swell.

'You feel like satin,' he told her huskily. 'The purest, richest satin ever made.'

And then his thumb brushed against her nipple, causing it to ache and throb so much that she couldn't suppress the taut moan of need that burned her throat.

His response was immediate, as he gathered her closer to him and started to caress the satiny flesh of her breasts with tender kisses, although it wasn't tenderness she wanted, Sara discovered on a sharp thrill of need. It was... It was...

She made a high sharp sound of release as his mouth opened over her nipple, her back arching, her head going back, her hands gripping him, digging into the muscles of his shoulders and neck as her whole body responded to the pulsing pleasure of his mouth suckling on her breast.

When she felt the sharp unexpected rasp of his teeth she shuddered, causing him to release her and to apologise.

Her eyes dark with arousal and new self-knowledge, she shook her head, telling him jerkily, 'No... It wasn't... It didn't... It wasn't pain.'

As she heard herself stammering the admission she went hot and cold with embarrassment, but Stuart quite obviously wasn't judging her as she was now judging herself, condemning her as wanton and over-demanding.

Instead he buried his face between her breasts, holding her so tightly against him that she could scarcely breathe, his voice rough and unfamiliar as he told her thickly, 'You're perfect, do you know that? *Perfect.* I still can't believe I've been lucky enough to find you. Sara...'

She felt the thrill of reaction engulf her as she heard the urgency in his voice. When he caressed her other breast as he had done the first, she stopped fighting against the sensations he was evoking, too bemused by the intensity of what she was feeling to realise that it was her own almost delirious words of pleasure and praise that were encouraging and inciting him to suckle on her tender, sensitive flesh until the pleasure he was giving her filled her so completely that she couldn't contain it any longer, crying out to him, reaching out to him.

The sensation of his mouth on her skin, hot, moist, so powerfully stimulating that everywhere he touched her she pulsed and burned, made her oblivious to everything other than the feelings she was experiencing.

She felt him moving her; felt the bed depress beneath their joint weight, felt his hand on her thigh, stroking gently upwards; felt the soft brush of his hair against her belly, the warmth of his in-drawn breath as he felt her tremble, her skin so sensitised by his touch that merely to feel his breath against it made her arch eagerly towards him.

'You're like velvet,' she heard him saying thickly to her as he had done before. 'Satin and velvet, so soft, so warm.'

She tensed, shock coiling through her as the slurred sound of his voice ceased and she realised that the heat, the pleasure, the need that made her both tremble with the tension of aching need, and at the same time relax into its narcotic delight, was caused by the delicate lap of his tongue against the most intimate part of her body.

Her brain, her mind; they were shocked and distraught not only by what he was doing but even more so by her reaction to it, but her body...

Her body overruled their fears and apprehensions, sinking into a languorous sensual delight in the pleasure he was giving her, the compliment he was surely paying her in wanting to pleasure her so intimately.

A compliment she knew instinctively she would like to return, she recognised dizzily as she moved against him, allowing her body to control her reactions, her responses, so that when she moved against him Stuart moaned and turned his head, biting almost roughly into her thigh, and then pulling her down against him so that he could tell her huskily, 'The way you react to me is driving me out of my head. My God, how could you ever, ever have imagined that you weren't desirable? You're the most desirable woman I've ever known.'

He was cupping her face, kissing her fiercely...demandingly, his body hard and eager against her own, its movements rhythmic and erotic.

'Sara, I never intended things to go this far. I should stop. I should...'

She silenced him by biting sharply into his bottom lip and then wrapping her arms around him, opening herself so completely and deliberately to him that she felt the shudder that ripped through him as he acknowledged the wanton temptation of her body.

To think of stopping now, to think of being denied the satisfaction her body craved.

She moved her hips and arched her back, moaning frantically as she felt the tormenting thrust of his tongue within her mouth, wanting, needing with all of her body and her soul to have that deeper, more powerful, more intimate thrust of his flesh within hers, so much so that when he finally moved her, caressed her, covered her with the heat and weight of his body, and then finally entered her, she cried out with frantic need, arching to meet his careful controlled movements, wrapping her body around his, raking her nails against his back, overwhelming him so much with the sheer intensity of her need that he cried out to her that he was afraid he might hurt her and that he could no longer control his reaction to her.

She had read enough, heard enough to know what she might expect to feel, but the actual intensity of her own experience, her own fulfilment was so overwhelming that she cried out almost in panic at the sheer awe-inspiring power of it, her body trembling so much in its aftermath that she felt as physically incapable of movement as though she had lost complete control of her nervous system.

She was, she discovered with shock, crying, or at least not crying so much as having tears simply seep from her eyes, and she wouldn't even have realised it if it hadn't been for the fact that Stuart was tenderly licking them away, as he held her and soothed her, praising her, comforting her, making her realise on a small forlorn surge of depression that for him this was a familiar experience... that this was not for him, as it was for her, something so new, so fresh, so powerful that at the height of it she had actually felt as though she had become immortal. Now, with the immediacy of her passion spent, she felt embarrassed, insecure...ashamed of the wanton way in which she had behaved.

She tried to pull away from him, but Stuart was holding her too tightly.

A lassitude, a physical and emotional exhaustion unlike anything she had ever experienced before crept over her, easing her inexorably towards sleep.

She tried to fight it, to will herself to stay awake, but it was impossible. Her last awareness before she lost her fight to stay awake was of Stuart gently cupping her face, and kissing her, not with passion or desire, but with tenderness and a whole host of other emotions her confused senses could only register impossibly as a mixture of warmth, pleasure, intimacy and understanding, the whole of which somehow went to make up the single word that encompassed them all, and which shimmered dangerously, luring her into hazard and danger; and that word was 'love'.

But Stuart didn't love her. Stuart loved someone else. Stuart...

She drew a deep uneven breath and, before she had time to release it, had fallen asleep.

The morning sun woke her, slanting across the bed, warming her closed eyelids, making her move drowsily and languorously, the narcotic of sleep still anaesthetising her senses until she opened her eyes and realised where she was.

She sat bolt upright in horror and stared towards the window. Not her own bedroom window at

home, but Stuart's bedroom window. Soon to be
their bedroom window. Her throat felt tight with
shock and disbelief.

She must have slept very deeply, she realised, because she was wrapped like a mummy in a quilt.
There was also only one pillow on the bed, and
only one imprint on it—her own. Which meant that
either Stuart had sensitively and caringly realised
how self-conscious, how diffident, how confused
she would feel if she woke up and found him lying
there next to her, or he had simply not wanted to
stay with her. She shivered a little.

Someone—and it could only have been Stuart—
had folded her clothes neatly for her and placed
them on a chair. There was, she discovered, a flask
on the table beside the bed, and a note propped up
against it.

She picked it up nervously and read it.

> Coffee in flask. Telephoned your mother last
> night to tell her that, having shared a bottle
> of wine over our supper, neither of us felt
> it would be wise to drive and that you were
> spending the night here.

There was nothing else, no message of love...no
mention of the intimacies they had shared...but
at least he had taken the trouble to telephone her
parents, although really there was no reason why
he should not have woken her up and sent her
home, except...

Except that had he done so her sense of rejection
would have been so intense...so painful...

Had he known that? Had he guessed that...?

That what? What was there, after all, for him to guess, to know, other than that where he was concerned she seemed to have a disastrous tendency to lose all self-control, to become so overwhelmed by desire, by need...? She blushed a little, remembering the previous night. Her body felt different—not in the classical sense, there was no discomfort, nothing of that order—but there *was* a difference: a languorousness, a ripeness almost, as though against her will, against her shock at its wantonness, it clung secretly and sensuously to its memories of the previous night, to its knowledge that it was after all just as much a finely tuned and receptive instrument of passion as anybody else's, even women of Anna's ilk. That she was not incapable of experiencing desire...nor, it seemed, of arousing it.

Whatever fears and apprehensions marriage to Stuart might hold, a lack of sexual compatibility between them could no longer be one of them.

Was that why he had done it? Was that why? Had she perhaps misinterpreted his response to her after all? Could it have been a deliberate ploy to soothe her fears? Was it possible for a man to pretend...to fake?

Shakily she extracted herself from the duvet, acknowledging that there was no point in looking for flaws...for doubts. That if she must dwell on what had happened then she would be far better employed in dwelling on something which she could not doubt nor question. Such as her own pleasure.

She gave a tiny shiver as she opened the door to the bathroom.

The small room had been panelled in keeping with the bedroom, the plain traditional white suite replacing the tawdry sanitaryware which had been there previously. Coil matting covered the floor, prickling her bare feet slightly. The room had a new, slightly harsh smell about it.

She closed her eyes, trembling as she remembered how last night she had breathed in the scent of Stuart's skin, how she had stroked and kissed it, tasting its texture, its heat... its scent with her tongue.

Her body went hot, a small ache starting up inside her. Angrily she ignored it, turning on the shower, and trying not to wince as she stepped under its icy sting.

Half an hour later she was downstairs in the study, trying to work.

She hadn't wanted any breakfast. She had rung her parents and spoken to her mother, who seemed to think there was nothing out of the ordinary in her having spent the night under Stuart's roof.

'I'm just on my way out,' her mother told her. 'I want to have a word with Gwen Roberts, to check the flowers for the church.'

Sara replaced the receiver. She had the house to herself. Before coming down, she had studied the bed, her fingers drifting gently over its carving. Her wedding gift. The kind of gift that a man might make for a woman whom he greatly loved. She smiled bitterly to herself. The love was there, self-evident in the workmanship, but it was not love for her; it could not be... rather it must be love for the house. The bed wasn't so much a gift for her as a gift for the manor. She tried not to imagine how she might feel if Stuart had actually felt that kind of emotion for her, that depth of love, that intensity of commitment.

She was not going to cry, she told herself fiercely. After all, what was there to cry for? She was marrying a man with whom she had every chance of building a safe, secure life; she knew him well enough now to know that he would make her a loyal and caring husband, that he would be a loving father to their children, that he would share his life with her. That he would... Love her? Hardly... But then why should she want him to when...? She froze as she heard a car drawing up outside, and hurried into the kitchen, automatically assuming that it must be Stuart, hesitating only when she reached the kitchen, worrying at her bottom lip as she acknowledged that he might not be best pleased to find her standing here in the kitchen waiting for him.

She was just walking into the study when the kitchen door opened and a totally unexpected but very familiar male voice called her name.

It wasn't the voice she had expected. It wasn't Stuart's voice.

She turned round, scarcely able to believe her ears, her hand going to her throat, her whole body registering her shock.

'Ian...'

'So you *haven't* forgotten me?'

It was all there, the confidence, the self-assurance, the vanity and the self-love, and as he walked towards her she could only wonder that she had never noticed them so intensely before, but had simply accepted them...accepted them humbly and with worshipful adoration.

Now it was different. Now it was as though the proverbial scales had fallen from her eyes; as though she were a completely different person, and where she had previously felt acceptance she now felt revulsion...revulsion and irritation.

'My poor sweet. How you must have suffered. But that's all over now... I've realised my mistake, and I'm here to eat humble pie, although you must admit that Anna was an alluringly tempting little morsel. Small wonder that I was momentarily dazzled. But that's all over now.'

He had followed her into the study, and her nose wrinkled in distaste at the strong smell of his aftershave, far too overpowering in such a small space.

He was, she realised with some dislike, standing far too close to her as well, invading her personal space to a degree that was not merely impolite, but which also bordered on the sexually intimidating.

She moved away from him immediately, impelled to do so by her need to put some distance between them, and wished she had not as he followed her closely, pushing the door to behind him.

As he came towards her, she had to remind herself that *this* was Ian... Ian whom she had loved for almost all of her adult life. Ian who...

Ian...who had rejected, spurned her...who had used her, if not sexually then certainly emotionally and mentally, even if he had done so with her acceptance, her connivance almost. Another man, a better man, knowing he could not return her love, would have firmly severed the connection between them immediately he had guessed her feelings. A man like . . . a man like Stuart, for instance. She swallowed hard, confused and bewildered by her thoughts, trying to tell herself that she ought to be feeling joy, happiness, delirium almost. Ian was here. Ian wanted her . . . Ian was telling her that it was over between him and Anna, that he wanted her to return to London with him immediately, that he wanted . . .

She took a deep breath and interrupted his assured, almost mocking flood of meaningless assurances.

'Ian, I can't come back to London with you. I'm getting married.'

'Married?' He raised a taunting eyebrow. 'Oh, yes, your father did say something of the sort. Something or other about you marrying some bucolic type who lives locally. But honestly, my dear, can you really and truly see yourself living here? You're a city creature. You're like me. You and I——'

'No, I'm not,' she told him shakily. 'I'm not like you at all, Ian.'

He looked at her; he was growing irritated now, annoyed with her for refusing to succumb to his charm, his needs. She wondered cynically why it was he wanted her back—to soothe his ego, or to sort out the mess in the office?

'All right, so I made a mistake,' he was saying now, his voice losing its polish, its allure, sharpening . . . hardening . . . grating on her, she recognised with a small stab of guilt. She didn't want to listen to him, didn't want to hear what he had to say. Didn't even want him here at all, she admitted.

In fact what she wanted...what she wanted most of all was to close her eyes and discover when she opened them again that Ian had gone and that Stuart had taken his place.

The shock of her own admission threw her. She wanted Stuart...preferred Stuart...needed Stuart... Loved Stuart. But no...how could that be? How could she?

'All right, Sara,' Ian was saying snappily, 'So you want your pound of flesh; you want to see me grovelling. Well, I can't blame you for that, I suppose, although I had rather hoped you'd be above that sort of thing. You of all people know how vulnerable I am, how much I need——'

'To have your ego massaged,' she supplied drily for him.

She watched as the blue eyes turned cold and merciless. 'Anna was right about you,' he told her venomously. 'You are a cold, sexless creature. A woman who isn't really a woman at all. You're getting married, you say? Why, I wonder? You can't possibly love him.'

'Can't I? Why not? Because I was once foolish enough to love you? That's over, Ian. I think it was over the day Anna told me that you'd known all along how I felt about you. I knew then that I'd loved not a man but a mirage. Stuart is worth a hundred of you.'

'And you *love* him? You're lying, Sara. I know you. I know your type. You love me. You always have done and you always will——'

'No!' she interrupted him vehemently. 'I don't love you, Ian.'

'Oh, yes, you do, and on your wedding night when you're lying cold and unresponsive beside your farmer, it will be me you'll want... me——'

'No,' she told him again, and then lifted her head, and said something she could never in a thousand lifetimes have ever imagined herself saying to anyone, never mind to Ian. 'You're quite wrong, Ian, and do you know *how* I know you're wrong? Last night Stuart and I were lovers. I'd been so afraid, more afraid of anything than I've been in my whole life. And do you know *why* I was afraid? I was afraid because of you. Not because I once loved you, but because of the way you'd hurt me... derided me, allowed Anna to hurt me so cruelly and so fundamentally that I was terrified that she was right; that I was incapable of arousing desire within any man. But then Stuart touched me... showed me...' She took a deep breath, her voice trembling as she continued bravely, 'Stuart gave me a pleasure I'd never dreamed could exist for anyone, never mind for me, and he gave me that pleasure generously and freely.'

She felt tears sting her eyes and dashed them away with the back of her hand.

'And because of that... because of that, even if I *didn't* love him, even if I *still* loved you—which I do not—I would still stay with him, marry him, because you see, Ian, when it comes down to it,

Stuart is the most complete, the most whole, the most stable human being I've ever known. Beside him you're nothing but a tawdry, gimcrack imitation of all that a man should be.'

'My God, you *do* love him, don't you? All that after one night of sex. He must be good. Tell you what, old girl, if I were you I'd be wondering how he got to be so good. If he's got that kind of taste for women . . . for sex, ask yourself. How long is he going to be satisfied with you? He might marry you, but my bet is he won't be faithful to you. Are you sure you don't want to change your mind?'

She had turned her back on him. 'No, Ian, I won't change my mind.'

She didn't move until she actually heard his car driving away, and then when she tried to move she discovered she was so tense that all she could do was stand there and shake.

She felt sick, her head was starting to pound, she felt weaker than she had ever felt before in her life and at the same time she felt stronger.

She loved Stuart. It amazed her that until she had actually framed the words, said them, she had really not known, and yet last night, and even before last night, some deep inner core of her *must* have known, must have known and must have kept the knowledge hidden from her. Her tremors increased.

She couldn't marry Stuart now, of course. It wouldn't be fair, to either of them. It had worried her enough when she had simply thought she desired him more than he desired her, but now that she knew the truth . . .

She gnawed on her bottom lip. How was she going to tell him...convince him? And then she realised that Ian's visit provided her with the perfect excuse.

There was no need for Stuart to know the truth, for her to embarrass them both by revealing it; she could simply tell him that Ian's engagement was over, that he wanted her back, that he realised... Her throat closed against the revulsion that filled her body at the thought of even implying that she still loved Ian. She had clung to her delusions for so long that she was actually beginning to wonder if perhaps she had in fact stopped loving him a long time ago, but had simply never allowed herself to admit it. That would certainly explain her lack of physical desire for him, her belief that sexually she was not the type of woman to feel intense desire; a fiction which her reaction to Stuart had very quickly revealed as such.

She didn't have long to wait for Stuart's return. The Land Rover came clattering into the yard just, as luck would have it, as she was making some coffee.

She watched, her throat taut with pain, her heart aching, as Stuart strode across the yard towards the door. How would he take it? Would he be angry or would he just incline his head in that way he had and listen to her, calmly letting her go?

She discovered as she picked up her mug that her hands were trembling too much for her to hold it.

He came into the kitchen and looked across the room towards her.

'Stuart... Stuart, there's something I have to tell you.'

He waited in silence, not helping her, but not hindering her either.

'It's... It's... I can't marry you after all,' she told him shakily, not daring to look at him.

'I see.' There was a short pause. She tensed as he kicked off his Wellingtons and came across the kitchen, but before he reached her he stopped beside the table, pulling out a chair and sitting down.

'Do you mind if we talk this over sitting down?' he asked her, flexing his back with a small wince. 'My back's killing me. The bed in the spare room isn't the most comfortable one I've ever slept on, and I've been transplanting some saplings all morning. This sudden change of heart—of mind should I say?—it wouldn't have anything to do with last night, would it?'

Sara stared at him. 'No...no, of course not,' she assured him truthfully, and then flushed brilliantly scarlet as she realised how misplaced her vehement assurance was, and how inappropriate, but fortunately he seemed not to be aware of her self-betrayal, asking her instead,

'So why, then?'

This was it. She gripped her hands together, praying for the strength to lie convincingly to him. 'I...I had a visitor this morning.' She wanted to turn away from him, but realised too late that since she was seated opposite him she could scarcely do so.

'Er—it was Ian, to be exact... His engagement to Anna is finished. He's asked me... He wants

me to go back to him, and I...well, you already
know that I...that I...' She swallowed hard, finding
it almost impossible to voice the lie but knowing
she had to do so.

'That you what?' Stuart prompted her. 'That you
love him?'

She nodded, unable to continue.

'Odd. Especially when less than an hour ago I
myself heard you telling him that you most
assuredly did not love him and that you had no
intention of returning to London with him.'

Sara couldn't believe her ears. 'You heard? But
you couldn't... You...'

'I came back for the Land Rover keys... The
study door wasn't properly closed. I had already
seen the strange car outside. I didn't mean to
eavesdrop, but when I heard what he was saying to
you...'

He paused and Sara asked weakly, 'How long?
How much...? No, Stuart. Please don't,' she
protested huskily, as he got up out of his chair and
came towards her, his intention plainly written in
his eyes.

'Well, let's just say I was there long enough to
hear you say you loved me,' he told her tenderly,
as he reached for her, almost lifting her bodily out
of her chair and wrapping her in his arms, her
protests and denials smothered against his mouth
as he started to kiss her.

'Those words were almost the sweetest music I'll
ever hear.'

'Almost?' she mumbled helplessly against his
mouth. 'But——'

'The sweetest ones will be when we stand up in church together and you say "I will". Sara, Sara, I can't believe it, even now,' he groaned, kissing her fiercely and hugging her. 'You love me... I admit I'd hoped that with time and patience one day you might, but to hear you tell him...'

'Stuart, please, it isn't any use... I still can't marry you. Not when I know that you love someone else. You must see that it wouldn't be fair to either of us.'

'Me, love someone else?' He had stopped kissing her and had moved back slightly from her so that he could look down into her eyes. 'What on earth do you mean? Of course I love you. I have done from the moment I set eyes on you. It was as if I was being pole-axed... as if I was being hit by a falling redwood... the shock of it damn near killed me. One moment I was a sane, well-adjusted man of thirty-odd, going about his business; the next... The next, I'd taken one look at you and known, known immediately and irrefutably that my life was changed for all time.'

'Stuart...that can't be true. You told me yourself there had been someone...Sally.'

'Sally?' He looked totally bewildered. 'The only Sally I know is my sister-in-law, and as for there being someone else... There have been some relationships, I admit, relationships which I might have thought might lead to a permanent commitment, but there's never been a woman who's made me feel the way you make me feel. If I implied otherwise, it wasn't intentional.'

'You told me...you said...you implied that you knew what it was like to love someone and know that love couldn't be returned. I assumed it must be someone in Canada—that you'd bought the house for her but that she'd rejected you.'

'Canada? Never! You... Wait a minute.' He started to smile. 'Ah, the night we met when I looked at you and knew, knew you were the one. You were the woman I wanted, needed. It threw me a bit. And then you told me about Ian.'

'Ian.' She gave a small shudder. 'I can't believe now that I ever even liked him, never mind loved him. He's so shallow, so, so...'

'Unimportant to us and our future together,' Stuart suggested lovingly. 'Shall we just consign him to the past, and close the door on him, then? I can certainly think of far more important things we can talk about.'

'Such as?' Sara asked him dizzily.

'Such as how it felt to hold you in my arms last night, to hold you and make love to you, and how much I want to repeat that experience...so much so that I don't think I can wait another three weeks.'

'You really did make that bed for me, didn't you?' Sara marvelled, blushing a little as she heard the passion, the desire in his voice.

'I really made it for both of us,' he teased her, 'but yes, the carving was for you. A symbol of my love...a labour of love, if you like. Last night...I didn't mean it to happen, you know. I just wanted to reassure you, to show you that you were wrong, that you *were* desirable, but when I touched you...'

She felt him shudder. 'I just couldn't control my reaction to you, my need for you, my love, and then when you were so...so inviting...so responsive, I wanted to stay with you, to wake up with you in my arms, but I was afraid of crowding you, of pressing too much intimacy on you too soon. I still couldn't bring myself to wake you up and send you home, though. If I couldn't have you in my bed, then at least I could keep you under my roof. I love you, Sara.'

'I love you,' she responded, the words blurred and softened by the pressure of his mouth.

'Well, no one could possibly doubt that they're in love,' Margaret commented softly to Ben as they stood side by side, watching as Sara and Stuart emerged from the church, his arm around her, her face turned up towards his as he paused to kiss her.

The bells pealed an exultant message of joy, the pageboys protested shrilly that they wanted to change into their jeans, the bride's mother dabbed at her eyes, the sun shone and the happiness of the occasion spilled out across the ancient churchyard, enveloping both the guests and the onlookers.

'When Sara first told me she was going to marry Stuart, I...' Margaret broke off, shaking her head. 'I've never seen her look so happy...so...so fulfilled.'

'Don't say that too loudly,' Ben warned her with a grin, adding, when she gave him a puzzled look, 'the fulfilment bit isn't supposed to happen until tonight, or am I being old-fashioned?'

'Hopelessly,' Margaret told him forthrightly, kissing him fondly on the cheek.

'Still love me?' Stuart murmured softly in Sara's ear.

She turned her head, giving him such a luminous and betraying look of adoration that his heart turned over in his chest.

'Do you really need to ask?' she whispered back.

'Mmm ... No, not really.'

'Do *you* love *me*?'

'Just wait until tonight, when I can show you as well as tell you.'

Sara flushed a little and laughed, and then whispered teasingly, 'Think you'll still love me in four months' time when I'm starting to look like a balloon?'

For a moment she thought he hadn't understood, but then the realisation dawned in his eyes, and his hand tightened on her arm as he demanded incredulously, 'Are you trying to tell me ...?'

'That I'm pregnant,' she supplied for him. 'Well, I'm not one hundred per cent sure, only ninety-nine point nine, but yes, I think so.'

She heard him laugh and groan at the same time as he exclaimed, 'What a time and place to choose to tell me!'

'I wasn't really sure myself until last night. I know it's a bit sooner than we'd planned.'

He must have caught the anxiety in her voice, because he pulled her to him and held her tenderly, telling her softly, 'It couldn't possibly be too soon as far as I'm concerned. I love you, Sara.' He bent his head and kissed her, oblivious to the amusement of the onlookers, and the arrested, disgusted look on the faces of the two small pageboys.

'Yuck,' the elder commented to his sibling. 'Look at that, soppy things...kissing!'

'Mmm. Soppy things indeed,' Margaret murmured to Ben, 'And long may they continue to be so. Which reminds me...'

'Have a little respect, woman,' Ben urged her, trying not to laugh. 'Remember this is sacred ground.'

'That doesn't seem to be stopping Stuart and Sara,' his wife pointed out sweetly to him.

'No, it doesn't, does it?' he agreed, his smile broadening, and he followed Stuart's example and took his wife in his arms.

Harlequin is proud to present our best authors and their best books. Always the best for your reading pleasure!

Throughout 1993, Harlequin will bring you exciting books by some of the top names in contemporary romance!

In June,
look for
*Threats and
Promises* by

BARBARA

DELINSKY

The plan was to make her nervous....

Lauren Stevens was so preoccupied with her new looks and her new business that she really didn't notice a pattern to the peculiar "little incidents"—incidents that could eventually take her life. However, she did notice the sudden appearance of the attractive and interesting Matt Kruger who *claimed* to be a close friend of her dead brother....

Find out more in THREATS AND PROMISES ... available wherever Harlequin books are sold.